THE SUN, THE SIN
& THE SHAME

THE SUN, THE SIN & THE SHAME

LEIGH McKNIGHT

I thank God for allowing me to continue this journey of writing the books that I love to write. To my family, friends and all those who have supported me through the years and continue to support me. I appreciate you, and I thank you very much.

Table of Contents

THE SUN, THE SIN & THE SHAME

CHAPTER 1

If you lay down with the devil, you will wake up in hell. That thought rolled around inside Mitch Hardin's head like the numbered balls in the rotating barrel that lottery officials use to pick the winning lottery number. Mitch fumed as he sat on the couch staring at the closed door that his wife had slammed behind her in one of the worst displays of her angry tirades he had ever experienced. And, he had experienced many of these tirades from her, some so demeaning and vicious, they left him feeling inferior, ashamed, emasculated, but mostly, those tirades left him feeling like a piece of shit. Mitch ran his fingers down over his face and let out a long sigh. Clearly, he was getting sick and tired of his wife's unfounded attack on him but what could he do about it. He loved her.

Mitch got up, walked over to the bar in their hotel suite and angrily snatched a glass from the rack, dropped in a few ice cubes from the ice chest and poured Bourbon over them. He took a large gulp from his drink glass and returned to his place on the couch, immersed in thoughts. Mitch, 40, and Kanile, 37, and his wife of twenty one years, were vacationing on Myrtle Beach in South Carolina. He loved his wife with every fiber in his being, more in fact than he thought was possible to love anyone. His biggest misconception was thinking she felt the same about him. Kanile had gone from treating Mitch like the loving husband he was to treating him like a sugar daddy. She seemed to only love Mitch when he satisfied all her lavish wants. He had begun to feel like he had been loving and married to a stranger all these years. Coming to terms with that, Mitch's confidence waned, his self-esteem took a major hit, much like the proverbial kick in the stomach. Kaline was the definition of evil. Mitch began to realize that trying to satisfy Kaline's every whim was turning his life into a living, breathing, fire-burning hell.

When did Mitch and Kanile's lives changed so much? He knew exactly when their lives began to unravel. Three years ago, Kanile met and became friends with Tracy and Vanessa who were married to doctors with thriving practices and who provided them with everything their hearts desired. Shortly after their friendship began, Kanile quit her job as a dental hygienist and became a lady of leisure in imitation of Tracy and Vanessa's lives, her now two best friends.

Keeping up with the Joneses is never easy. Anyone who tries and doesn't have the means to do so, knows it. The Joneses could do all the things that money could buy; trips to foreign exotic locales, impulsive weekend getaways, extravagant shopping sprees along with expensive cars, big houses, and huge bank accounts. But, for the rest of us, those goodies were out of our reach and woe to many of those who tried. Mitch and Kanile tried keeping up with the Joneses but failed miserably and all they had to show for their efforts were overdrawn bank accounts, maxed out credit cards, and bill collectors blowing their phone up, attempting to collect overdue debts.

Mitch worked hard to please his wife but rarely succeeded with Kanile never failing to remind him in her derisive and emasculating way, verbally tearing him down for sport. Evan, their only child was 21, gainfully employed and living in California. Mitch spent every cent he earned on himself and his wife, but every cent he made was never enough for Kanile. She always wanted more and when she didn't get it, she would berate him for not providing her with the same lifestyle as those of her wealthy friends.

Mitch and Kanile argued again last night. The majority of their arguments were about money or in their case, the lack of it. Kanile had either spent too much of Mitch's hard earned money or she complained that Mitch didn't make enough money for her to spend. Mitch couldn't forget the harsh words Kanile hurled at him last night.

"If you made a decent salary, we wouldn't have to spend our one vacation a year in this third rate dive," she complained bitterly, in a sweeping gesture indicating their suite. "Myrtle Beach," she hissed, tossing her hair back. "Tracy and Vanessa's husbands take them to Paris, the Bahamas, really nice places," she said, drawing out the words 'really nice,' shooting daggers with her eyes at Mitch. "Just last month Tracy and Ed vacationed in Paris, while Vanessa and Irief spent a week in Vale, skiing, shopping enjoying fine dining," she continued on dreamingly. "But you, Mitch," she stood face to face with him, poking a finely manicured finger in his face, "The best you can do for your wife is Myrtle Beach, and you don't even provide me with a five star hotel. You put me in this dump. If you were any kind of man," she snarled with attitude, "you wouldn't have me in a place like this."

Okay their hotel wasn't the Four Seasons but it was exquisitely furnished with tasteful amenities; a Jacuzzi, a bar and a breathtaking view of the ocean.

"Give me a little while to make partner, baby, and I promise you things will be different," Mitch countered calmingly, placing his hands on her shoulders, trying to end his wife's complaints once and for all.

Kanile wasn't placated. "Don't you baby me," she roared, knocking Mitch's hands off her shoulders and looking at him furiously, motioning stop with her hand. "How long have you been telling me that? She screamed, waving a finger accusingly in his face. "You are a weak, pathetic excuse of a man who refuses to do right by your family."

Mitch's job as the real estate developer was extremely stressful, his salary wasn't bad, but Kanile was right, they only took one vacation a year. At the rate Kanile spent simply because Tracy and Vanessa did, it was a miracle they could afford one vacation a year.

Mitch looked down at his shoes. He had heard Kanile's complaints for a long time and knew she wasn't finished yet.

"I don't know why I bother," she continued to wail, shaking her head in despair and pacing the floor. "Talking to you just falls on deaf ears. Hell, I don't know why I married a loser like you when I could easily have married a doctor, a lawyer, or even a politician." Mitch had noticed a sly smile on his wife's face each time she mentioned the word 'politician' in her comments. "Anyone would've been a huge improvement over what I've got," she derided him, glancing hatefully at him over her shoulder.

Mitch tried to ignore the scathing comments on his character, but Kanile's tongue was her greatest weapon and she easily destroyed him with her words. "My friends spend lots of money all the time and they never seem to run out, but our bank account is none existent. Bill collectors are calling, delinquent bills filling up the mailbox." She lifted her hands in exasperation, spinning around in circles. "What am I supposed to do? When is my damn ship coming in?"

Mitch had watched Kanile's dramatics; putting her hand to her head and rolling her eyes towards the ceiling as if the Creator would come down from the clouds and give her the answers she was looking for. Mitch had thought, a little bitterly, that she could get a job and help pay the bills that she almost single-handedly created, but he couldn't say that to his wife. She was the woman he had promised to always love and take care of, and he took his vows seriously and wasn't going back on his word now.

Meeting her gaze with a determined look, he said, "I am doing the best I can."

She spun quickly towards the mirrored vanity. "Humph, well your best ain't good enough." She yanked out a drawer and begun fumbling through her vast amount of makeup; combs, brushes, hair products. I don't ask for much. For once I wish we could just have a fabulous time and not have to worry about how we're gonna eat the next day," she finished her wishful thinking by shooting her husband a demeaning look.

Mitch caught her expression and going to take a seat on the couch, offered hopefully, "Maybe next year."

Finding the desired items, Kanile slammed them on top of the dresser with a clatter. She turned from the mirror. "That's what you said last year and the year before that. Should I go on?" Flying into a frenzy again, unleashing in rapid procession of more verbal assaults on Mitch. "You are such a freaking loser. No good for anything. I can't believe I married you" all the while, furiously applying makeup to her beautiful mocha complexion.

Kanile was a pretty woman; oval shaped face, high cheek bones, large dark brown eyes, and a small keen nose over luscious shapely lips. She had an hour glass body that had totally captivated Mitch from the moment he met her. Unfortunately, all that beauty couldn't hide Kanile's ugly attitude tonight.

She twisted her long jet black curly hair, allowing it to hang over one shoulder. She slipped into a very sexy, very short black dress that showed off her incredible five feet six figure.

"You're going somewhere?" Mitch inquired, getting up from the couch, seeing how his wife was dressed.

"Yes."

"Where are you going?"

Kanile turned her eyes back to him. "Out," she snarled.

Puzzled, Mitch eyed his wife. "Why didn't you say you wanted to go out?" he impatiently protested, glancing at his watch. "Do you know what time it is?"

"I don't care what time it is. I'm not on a time clock. I'm on vacation. If you want to call it that, she said, getting a quick dig in. "I'm going to find some fun."

Completely exhausted from all the hours he'd spent working before going on this trip, Mitch slumped his shoulders in surrender, moving over to his wife. "Just give me tonight and we'll do whatever you want tomorrow. Come on, I'll put on some music, make us a couple of drinks, then we can make crazy love like we used to." He grinned shyly.

"You're so predictable, no spontaneity." Kanile gave herself a final look. Satisfied with what she saw in the mirror, she said, "Thanks, but no thanks." Then, she walked toward the door.

Since Kanile insisted on going out tonight, Mitch decided to accompany her. "Alright, let me throw on something and I'll go with you." He was about to make a move toward the bedroom to change when Kanile stopped him in his tracks.

"No, you get your rest. I'm going out alone, and if I'm lucky tonight, I'll find a real man this time around." Ignoring the pain on her husband's face, Kanile walked up to the door and paused, calling over her shoulder, "Don't wait up, dear."

Mitch frowned deeply. "Kanile," he called out as the door slammed shut behind her. He threw both hands in the air, then walked over to the couch, slumping down hard. He stayed there for a long while before making his way to the portable bar where he poured himself some Bourbon over ice cubes and took several huge swallows. Mitch nursed one drink after another and had quit counting after the third. Around 1:00 am with no sign of his wife's return, he went to bed. When he awoke at 3:45 the next morning laying across the bed fully clothed, he realized he was still alone in their suite. Mitch didn't wake again until late morning. He looked around the room. The dress Kaline wore last night lay on the side of the bathtub, and her shoes were on the bathroom floor but she was not there.

* * *

Wanting to calm down after leaving Mitch alone in their suite, Kaline had walked down the brown carpeted hallway to the elevator. She had no idea where she was heading but knew she had to get away for a while. Truth be told, she also knew she'd been a bitch toward Mitch. He didn't deserve to be spoken to in such a vile way, the cruelty she heaped upon him, but she was too angry, too frustrated and too disappointed how her own life had turned out, to admit that to Mitch's face.

If only Kaline hadn't gotten caught up wanting to live the high life! Only she knew how much she regretted quitting her job, and now she was just too old to try and make it in that rat race. The younger generation and the veterans would be just too much competition for her to really find a good job that paid good money.

Kaline knew eventually she would have to apologize to her husband for her behavior, but not right now. She was still too upset; frustrated with her unemployment and Mitch's inability to maintain the lifestyle she demanded.

Of course it wasn't all Mitch's fault, but he was the easiest one to blame. Surely she shouldn't have left him the way she did and she really should be giving him the respect he deserved but just look at tonight for example. The vacation was already a cheaper version of what she had envisioned, but even more infuriating was that Mitch wanted to spend their vacation cooped up in a hotel room…and not even an elegant, expensive room. Hell to the no! She wasn't some old woman to be put in a corner and be expected to stay there. She was not that girl. Kaline intended to have a lot of fun on her vacation, irregardless of what Mitch wanted.

When the door opened, Kaline entered the semi-crowded elevator with a noisy group of people who were talking about going to some nearby club to party. When the elevator doors opened on the first floor, the group exited and walked through the hotel lobby out onto the street. Deep in thought, Kaline exited the elevator and began to walk slowly. Seeing the group from the elevator standing on the corner waiting for the light to change, Kaline picked up her pace and followed the group into a nightclub.

That Tuesday afternoon in July, the sun was high in the clear blue sky, the waves lapped up onto the sandy shore, and the beach was crawling with natives, sun seekers and visitors. As Mitch observed from his balcony, they appeared to have at least one thing in common. They were having hot fun in the summer time. Only Mitch wasn't having any fun. Kanile returned to the suite late last night, insisted he sleep on the couch and she left this morning before he awoke, so understandably, he wasn't having much fun. It definitely wasn't the vacation he'd hoped for.

Mitch dressed after a long shower. At a quarter past one, he began to wonder when his wife would return. He had become accustomed to Kanile's bad behavior when things didn't go her way; her angry outbursts, pouting and placing all the blame on him. But, last night had been different. Kanile had gone out alone and there was the added threat of her finding herself another man—a "real man this time," was how she had put it.

Feeling hunger pains, Mitch went to the refrigerator and removed a bottle of orange juice. Half way through the juice, he heard the suite door opening. Kanile ended a phone call as she entered the room, looking elegant in a Black two-piece bathing suit and straw wedge sandals. She tossed her hat, sunglasses and room key card on the dresser and dropped a towel on the foot of the bed.

"Where have you been?" Mitch asked, watching Kanile closely, clad in a tight skimpy bikini.

"I was taking a swim," she replied curtly, tossing her cell phone on the bed.

"I'm talking about last night. Where did you spend your night?" he demanded, staring at her from bloodshot eyes resulting from drinking too much and lack of sleep last night.

Kanile stared back at him angrily and her hands immediately flew to her hips. How dare he question anything she did to enjoy herself. Sometimes she felt Mitch was just too damn uptight, too overbearing. He just needed to chill out. She had no intentions of hanging out in a hotel room and listen to the ocean. Kaline preferred being in the ocean, preferably wrapped in a pair of strong arms.

"Answer me, Kanile," Mitch demanded.

She slowly removed her sandals before replying. "I was at a nightclub with some really cool people that I met in the elevator. They invited me to party with them, so that's where I was."

He inhaled sharply. "You're telling me you partied all night with a bunch of strangers?"

"Yeah. And?" She gave a helpless glance at the ceiling.
Mitch glared at his wife.

"We had a great time. It was off the chain." She gave him a sly look.

"I just bet it was," he mumbled sarcastically.

"Let it go, Mitch," she held up her hand, fingers opened like a stop sign.

Mitch blinked unbelievingly. His voice rose, "You were out all night partying with a bunch of strangers and when questioned, all you can say…"

Kanile interrupted him, screaming, "I don't give a damn what you think or how you feel about what I do. We weren't doing anything here but sitting around, acting like we are a hundred years old. Well, no thank you. My intention was to come here and have a good time while I'm on vacation and that's exactly what I did so chill out will you." Kanile removed a comb from her hair and tossed it on the dresser as her long dark locks fell down around her shoulders. "Besides," she added, "weren't you and I strangers when we first met? But we are no longer strangers, are we?" She smirked.

Mitch read the implication in her statement and for a moment he became speechless. How could she throw that back in his face when she herself was a willing participant? For the record, she was the instigator. Quickly, Mitch recalled how he met Kanile. They were at a college frat party and she was on the arm of a much sought after jock who was the star player for their football team. She was engaged to be married to him when her eyes lit on Mitch. He had recently transferred from Brown University to Temple so he was the new senior on the block. Kanile waited until her fiancé left to hook up with his jock friends before slowly making her way to Mitch to ask his name. After that she made it her business to find out all she could about him and be in the same places he was. One thing led to another and before long she had broken off her engagement with her former boyfriend to enter into a relationship with Mitch. All of this flitted across his mind as his wife turned the knife deeper into his aching gut.

"I rest my case." Kanile smirked deviously.

He set his jaw because she'd already hit a nerve, a raw one. Mitch shook his head, trying to clear the unpleasant images racing around in his mind. "Have you eaten?" he asked. Mitch could tell Kaline was still angry and wanted to defuse the situation. He was feeling as pathetic as Kaline had told him over and over and that wasn't a good look.

She laughed with bitterness, her eyes an angry brown pool of spite. "Don't worry about me," she said, coolly, making her way to the bathroom. "I'm going to take a shower and a nap because I am going out with some friends tonight."

"Some of our friends are here?" Mitch wanted to know.

Kanile stopped short of entering the bathroom. She turned and looked at Mitch, her lips curled in a devilish grin. "No one you know, dear. These are people I met last night."

For the first time since he'd known his wife, he looked at her with suspicious and distrustful eyes, and though he was angry, he said, "I thought tonight was going to be our date night."

"Those were your plans, Mitch, not mine," she said, stepping into the bathroom. When Kanile came out of the bathroom naked, throwing her bathing suit on the couch, she picked up the conversation where she left off. "The people I met last night were great. I don't know about you, but I am going to make the most of my time."

"Am I at least invited this time?"

Kanile shook her head. "I don't think you would like this crowd."

"What's going on, Kanile? I thought we came here to unwind and do some things together."

"Go to hell, Mitch," Kanile said, got into bed and turned her back towards him.

"Yeah, I love you too," Mitch mumbled, under his breath. He put the half emptied bottle of orange juice back in the refrigerator and shaking his head in disappointment, he left the room.

Mitch drove around until he found an IHOP. He ordered grits, scrambled eggs, turkey sausage, bacon and toast. He had coffee and another glass of orange juice.

After eating heartily and smoking two cigarettes, he went back to their suite, only to find his wife had left again.

"That didn't take long," he mumbled to himself, dropping his keys onto the bar.

Mitch pulled a beer from the refrigerator and went out onto the terrace to wait for Kanile. As he settled in one of the chairs and looking out across the ocean and the beach below, he smoked one cigarette after another. Kaline's treatment of Mitch was getting worse. Even when he did his best, she didn't appreciate his efforts. Even with his salary, that was more than enough to comfortably take care of him and his wife. Had Kaline forgotten the unnecessary shopping sprees she went on simply because her friends did. What about the bedroom suite they purchased two years ago that was in perfectly good condition that she insisted on replacing. Kaline thought nothing of spending weekends with her girlfriends in Vegas where she gambled away nearly every dime that they did have. They lived comfortably, but Mitch's salary couldn't afford the luxurious lifestyles of their friends. That was the bottom line.

The late afternoon sun gleamed on the crystal choppy waters dotted with swimmers, people in small boats and jet skiers. As he now watched couples and listened to the sound of the surf rolling in and out, the only thoughts that occupied his mind were of his wife. Then, feeling completely exhausted, Mitch took one last drag from his cigarette before putting it out in the ashtray on the small table next to him. He got up from his chair and was about to reenter their suite when, suddenly, he saw her, a voluptuous young woman with a drop-dead, beach ready body slowly emerged out of the ocean. She was a vision of loveliness.

"Oh my God," he whispered, his eyes transfixed on the young woman. Mitch gripped the terrace railing, refusing to blink. He didn't want to miss a second gazing at the amazing creature. The bright red two piece bathing suit the young lady was wearing wrapped her luscious curves so wonderfully that it was almost sinful. Even from a distance, Mitch could tell the honey colored beauty was young. Perhaps half his age, still she was the most magnificent creature he'd ever seen, and he'd seen lots of beautiful women in his time.

As she walked out of the water onto the beach, water fell from her long copper hair that hung below her shoulders. Her movement was hypnotic; hips swaying provocatively, beckoning him. Finally, he blinked. Can anyone be that perfect or was she just a mirage? Perhaps, it was the amount of alcohol he'd consumer or the stress of the ongoing humiliation his wife levied on him before leaving him alone, again.

When the stranger looked towards Mitch, he was certain their eyes met and held until he forced his eyes away, trying to ignore thoughts he shouldn't be entertaining. Since he caught sight of the young woman, his mind had gone straight to the gutter…. and had lingered there. This wasn't like Mitch. Of course he looked good looking women and sure, he appreciated them, but he didn't always go around wondering what it would be like to have sex with them. After all, he was a married man who amazingly, despite his wife's demeaning and emasculating ways; he was still madly in love with her and he had no intention of betraying her.

Mitch looked in the young woman's direction again. After eyeing her another moment and becoming irritated by his own thoughts, he left the balcony and returned to the suite. He sat on side of the bed, reached for the remote and after turning the TV to the sports channel, he fell back against the pillows on the bed.

Sometime later, Mitch awoke, sat up in bed and looked at his watch. Nine o'clock. He'd slept away the entire afternoon.

"Kanile," Mitch called out. Then, upon seeing evidence that his wife had returned, changed for the evening and without informing him, she'd left again. Mitch was once again home alone. He picked up a pack of cigarettes and his lighter from the night table and wandered out on the terrace. He lit the cigarette, took one drag from it and leaned on the terrace railing. The ocean waters were really choppy now and the breezes were pleasant. He heard screams coming from below of swimmers enjoying the ocean and presumably each other. That's where he and Kanile should be he thought. Instead, she was out doing her own thing apart from him. Mitch put out his cigarette disgustedly. Everyone was having fun, enjoying themselves with their significant others and here he was all alone. He came to relax, unwind and have a good time. He was still sore from being left along by Kanile over and over. And he was sick of it. Well, two can play this game, Mitch thought heading to the bathroom. He quickly showered and dressed in a shirt and short pants before leaving the hotel. He drove their rental car around for a while until he found a club to his liking.

CHAPTER 2

The crowd at The Odyssey was mostly a younger sort but that didn't bother Mitch. All he wanted to do was to get out of the stifling hotel room. Kanile had left him alone long enough. Now it was time for him to get out and though he had only intended to get a sandwich and a couple of drinks to drown his sorrows before going back to their suite, it would be fun to see the look on Kanile's face when she returned and find him not there. The thought brought a warm smile to Mitch's face. Yeah, that would serve her right, he thought. Mitch noticed people on the dance floor, enjoying themselves, but there was one young lady who stood out in the crowd. He also noticed that his eyes weren't the only eyes that held the young woman in their sights.

Mitch's eyes briefly traveled from head to toe of the young woman. She was about 5 feet 8, gorgeous with beautiful copper hair piled on top of her head. She was wearing a sexy white dress that flared out before settling into folds against her shapely thighs and ending a good five inches above her knees, and her incredible long legs were anchored in strappy white shoes. It was obvious she loved to party as she laughed and danced with one partner on to the next.

Mitch sat at the bar and ordered a White Russian. He pulled from his short sleeve shirt pocket a pack of cigarettes and a lighter, he lit up a cigarette and placed the pack and lighter on the bar near him. He took a huge swallow of his drink before returning his glass to the bar.

Popular music filled the night spot with people dancing, talking and laughing while others were locked in their lovers' embrace, kissing passionately which caused Mitch to miss Kanile even more.

'A Whole Damn Year' by Mary J. Blige began to spill out of the large speakers near the dance floor. Mitch was a huge fan of hers and he began tapping his fingers on the bar to the tune.

His drink half finished, the bartender placed a fresh drink in front of Mitch.

"I didn't order that drink," Mitch protested, his glass in his hand.

"I know," the bartender replied. "The lovely young lady over there did," he nodded his head and Mitch looked in the direction the bartender indicated to see the young woman he had noticed earlier on the dance floor, sitting at a table with two couples. He lifted his glass in thanks to his beautiful benefactor. She smiled in return and he turned back to the bar. After a short while, the song, 'It Don't Hurt Now,' by

Teddy Pendergrass began blaring from the club's speakers and settled deep down into Mitch's brain. The record sounded just as good as when it was released years ago. *It would've been nice if Kanile had been there with him*, Mitch thought but he quickly banished that thought. To continue to think about Kanile would only serve to make him more unhappy.

Mitch finished his drink and started on the new one. Although his vacation definitely had turned into a fiasco, the consumption of alcohol had lightened his mood. He took another sip from his glass when he felt a gentle tap on his shoulder and heard a low sultry voice coming from behind him asked, "May I have this dance?"

Mitch turned to see the lady who bought him a drink standing next to him. He gave her another quick once over.

"Excuse me?" he mumbled his words as he set his glass back on the bar.

"I'd like to dance with you," she replied, resting her hand on top of his. He made no attempt to move her hand….or his.

"Thank you for asking, but I'm afraid I'm not much of a dancer," Mitch confided, shyly.

"You don't have to be," she said, her dark liquid eyes holding his hazel ones. "All you have to do is follow my lead." She held out an outstretched hand to him.

He gave her a hint of a smile. It'd been days since he really smiled but this young woman was about to change all that. What the heck, he thought. Wherever Kanile was, he was certain she was getting her groove on. Hadn't she even hinted as much?

He got up from the stool, took the young woman's hand and followed her to the small dance floor. Their bodies came together in sync. As the tune played, she pressed her body close to his where he could feel all her soft womanly parts resting against his hard firm body and as he held her close, the seductive fragrance of her perfume sent a powerful shudder through him.

"See. You are not so bad," she said, interrupting his thoughts, her mouth near his ear. He could feel her warm breath on his cheek.

"Really?"

"Oh yes. You've done this before," she teased.

"I suppose I'll do for an old man." Mitch wasn't egotistical or narcissistic so he was being honest about how he perceived himself. However, Mitch was a tall, exceedingly handsome man. His black hair was cut close to his scalp, his lips were full and sexy and the startling, drop-dead gorgeous hazel eyes that one could swim around in before getting completely lost, were surrounded by long thick lashes. He was well built; wide shoulders, nice abs and a rock hard broad chest that tapered down to a trim waist and narrow taut hips.

The young woman pushed her head away to look into his face.

"You are not old," she declared adamantly, allowing her eyes to roam up and down Mitch's body. Even beneath his brown shirt, she could detect nice broad shoulders and a strong, muscular back. His taut ass looked damn good in those beige short pants too. The man was hot from his killer eyes right down to his kick ass muscular legs that she noticed when he entered the club.

"You don't think so, huh?"

"No, I don't," she said, looking into his face, her eyes gleaming with vitality and excitement. He was a good looking man, she thought, and she didn't care how old he was.

One soulful ballad after another played and Mitch and his dance partner's body remained in sync on the dance floor. As he gazed into the eyes of this gorgeous young woman, he wondered why she was dancing with him when all those vital young men in the club were directing their attention to her, devouring her with their eyes whether they were alone or with someone.

"What are you thinking about?" she asked, pulling him from his reverie.

He blinked, "What? Oh, nothing," he said.

She called him on it. "You are lying," she stated confidently and unhesitant.

Mitch was taken aback by her boldness, but played it off. "You're calling me a liar when you don't even know me," he said, lightheartedly.

"I could say woman's intuition, but anyway, I don't have to know who you are to pick up on your thoughts." She smiled and added, "My name is Sophia, by the way. Sophia Hartford. My mother loved Sophia Loren, the actress, so when I came along, she named me after her."

"Sophia Hartford," he repeated her name. "Pleased to meet you, Sophia Hartford. Mitch Harding."

"Mitch Harding," she echoed his name in words resembling a tender caress, holding him like the arms of a lover. "Like in Mitch Miller?" she asked, giggling.

"Yep, but what would you know about Mitch Miller. He was long before your time."

"My parents listened to his music for years," Sophia said and as she looked up at him, he thought she was every bit as beautiful as her namesake. But, what was it about Sophia that seemed so familiar?

That record ended and the next record had an upbeat tempo. Mitch, still holding onto Sophia's hand, was about to lead her off the dance floor when Sophia said, "Ah come on. Let's get it crackin,' baby. Let's turn up." Before Mitch could protest, Sophia was dancing, sensuously circling him with sexy moves. It wasn't long before he was caught up in Sophia's energy and was dancing enthusiastically, displaying moves of his own, to the lively tune.

The next song was extremely high energy, causing a sensational stir among the crowd. It was difficult to determine who was dancing with whom. Some were doing the electric slide, some twerking, and Mitch noted that all men couldn't tear their eyes away from Sophia and were trying to get as close to her as they could.

Mitch leaned down and said against Sophia's ear, "You've got an audience."

"What are you talking about?" She gave him a pretended surprised look.

"Every man in the club has his eyes on you," Mitch said matter of fact.

"Really?"

"Don't pretend you didn't notice." He smiled down at her.

"I don't know what you're talking about," Sophie replied, throwing back her head, laughing.

How could she not, Mitch thought when every male's eyes in the club was on her. How could they not, Sophia was the most gorgeous woman Mitch had ever seen.

When the music stopped, they walked back to the bar. Mitch ordered another drink and a Cosmo for Sophie.

Mitch took a sip from his drink glass. "You look familiar."

"I get that a lot."

"You mean there is someone else out there who is as gorgeous as you?'

Then Sophie said, "I saw you watching me today."

Mitch blinked. "Excuse me!"

"Yes." She looked over the rim of her drink glass. "From your hotel balcony."

"From my hotel bal……" Mitch stopped in mid-sentence. It all came back to him now. He'd seen her earlier from his hotel balcony. "The red bikini," he stated.

Sophie pointed a finger at him. "You got it."

"You look different now."

"With my clothes on, you mean?" She snickered and took another sip of her drink.

Mitch grinned, revealing strong white teeth. Teeth Sophie was certain were capable of executing delicious, exciting yet indescribable pleasure, the kind of titillating pleasure a girl would welcome.

Mitch thought Sophia was gorgeous on the beach, but up close and personal, she was breathtaking from head to toe. Her body was banging, full of heart stopping curves, her face was right out of a dream and definitely her money shot. Her deep dark brown eyes were large and beautiful, her nose, small and narrow over full pouty lips looking like they were begging to be kissed, and dimples that should be registered as lethal weapons. Combine those attributes with porcelain honey colored skin gently kissed by the sun and you had one outrageously gorgeous woman who had the goods to compete with any model.

"Not that so much," he said. "I just thought you were gorgeous from afar with your hair bouncing around your shoulders and you're gorgeous now."

Sophia giggled. Then, she took another sip of her drink, leaped from the stool with her purse in hand, and flashing Mitch a bright smile, she said, "Why don't we get out of here and go do something dirty?"

"Did you just say, why don't we get out of here and go do something dirty?" Mitch said, taken aback at the nerve and sheer boldness of this young stranger.

Sophia nodded her head grinning up at Mitch.

"What does that mean?"

Sophia didn't reply. She chuckled, grabbed Mitch's hand and pulled him with her onto the dance floor where she whispered something to her girlfriend. The eyes of rejected and wanted-to-be suitors flashed with palpable lust toward Sophie and jealously towards Mitch as they hustled their way through the crowded club towards the door. Just before exiting the club, Sophia released Mitch's hand and dashed back to the bar for their drinks and she caught up with him at the door.

"What's this?" Mitch looked questioningly at Sophie.

"Our drinks." They exited the outer door.

Outside, the air was fresh and the breezes gently touched his face. Mitch took the drinks from Sophie's hands, emptied the content on the ground and set the glasses near the steps to the club.

Sophia was surprised. "Why did you do that?" she questioned.

"You don't get out much, do you?" Mitch said.

Sophia gave him an odd glance. "What?"

"I'll go get us some fresh ones," Mitch offered and turned to re-enter the club.

"Oh, never mind," Sophia said, clasping her hands together, excitement dancing in her pretty dark eyes and bouncing on her heels. "Let's go get some ice cream."

Mitch checked the time on his watch. Almost eleven. "I probably should be getting back to the hotel."

"And waste such a beautiful night? Come on."

Sophia impatiently grabbed Mitch's hand to lead him across the parking lot to the little bistro named Angelo's on the strip that was nestled between a spa and a jewelry store. Sophia took off at a run dragging Mitch behind her. She wanted to spend more time with Mitch in an intimate setting and catch the bistro before it closed. They reached the door slightly out of breath just as the owner was turning the OPEN sign around to read CLOSED.

"I'm closed," the owner, a small man with a crisp white apron with the name Angelo's blazoned in deep green on it over his clothing told them.

"Please! Can we come inside? We'd like an ice cream. We promise not to make a mess," Sophia pleaded with her big brown eyes.

"I'm sorry," the owner said, "but we are closed for the night," as he moved to walk away to finish cleaning.

Sophia beat on the door begging pitifully. The owner could not get the sad, disappointed look on her face out of his mind so he trudged back to the door and opened it just wide enough for them to squeeze through. Immediately Sophia launched herself at his chest giving him a big, tight hug.

"Thank you. Thank you. Thank you......." she squealed. Her youthful enthusiasm was very infectious.

The small man backed away sheepishly to return to stand behind the counter as he watched them pick out a small table near the window overlooking the beach. Mitch pulled out and held the chair for Sophia to be seated before moving around to take the seat across from her. She smiled and thanked him.

"What kind of ice cream would you like?" he asked.

"Mmmmm.....surpise me!"

"Ok. Wait a moment. I'll be back shortly". Mitch sprinted up to the counter to order a banana split with crushed pineapples, chocolate sauce, nuts and a cherry on top. He paid for his purchase and walked over to the old jukebox he spied as he walked into the quaint little eatery. Sophia drank in his chocolate body as he perused the music list. He hadn't heard this song in years. He put in a dollar in change and selected his choice. The sweet sound of Eugene Wild's 'Don't Say No Tonight' played in the almost quiet place. Mitch smiled then went back to the table. Though he was married he didn't want this time to end and he wanted to talk more with Sophia. She didn't make him feel like a heel. Mitch sat down across from her and leaned over the table to take her hand as he began talking.

"I hope you don't make it a habit of having a drink in a club, leaving it unattended then go back to reclaim it," he said, looking curiously at her. Sophia stopped bouncing around and gave Mitch her undivided attention. He continued lecturing her. "You are a gorgeous girl and there are some unsavory characters out here who are always up to no good. They'd like nothing more than to take advantage of a girl like you." Mitch paused and chuckled. "You saw those men in the club stripping you with their beady eyes, wishing for an opportunity. I'm not saying you shouldn't live your life. What's the point of it all if we don't take some risks? You just have to exercise some caution."

"Aye, aye, Sir, I have been sufficiently warned," Sophia teased him, laughing a deep throaty laugh before settling down to look into his mesmerizing eyes.

There was a moment of silence as they looked into each other's eyes before Mitch asked, "So tell me, Sophia, are you a local or are you vacationing here?"

Sophia answered, "Vacationing."

"What part of the world are you from?"

"New York."

"Aaah, the Big Apple. Such an exciting place to live."

"Do you live in New York?"

"No. My son did and we visited him quite often when he lived there and attended Hunter College. Evan graduated a year ago. He's out of my pocket, pays his own bills and he now lives in California." Mitch grinned when he said, "He's gonna be a movie star, he says."

"That's highly possible. All he has to do is want it badly enough and it definitely will happen for him."

"It's that simple, huh?" Mitch mocked Sophia with a doubtful glance.

"Absolutely," Sophia said with confidence, then added, "but the important thing is that your son is happy." Sadness covered Sophia's face for a moment as she looked out the window of the bistro. Then the brightness returned to her eyes when she said, "I've got friends in Cali. I intend to visit them this winter." Then she returned her attention to Mitch. "When you visited New York, did you like it?"

"Yeah, I did. We spent mostly long weekends there. We went to the famous Apollo Theater, we saw a number of Broadway shows, and we ate at some of the best restaurants."

"I think New York is the most amazing city in the world," Sophia said, giddy with excitement. "Have you had a Nathan's hot dog?"

"Oh man, I surely did. Those are the best hot dogs in the world. Don't know where or even if I've had a better hot dog," Mitch said and he and Sophia chuckled together.

"Why did you decide to vacation here in South Carolina?"

"A group of us went to the Bahamas last year. Africa, my friend back at the club, met this guy there, they kept in touch and agreed to meet here this week."

"What about you? You didn't meet your Mister Right there also?" Mitch surprised himself asking Sophia personal questions.

"None that piqued my interest." After a moment she looked at him and asked, "Who said anything about anyone meeting their Mister Right? We were just having some fun."

Mitch took that moment to change the conversation. "What do you do back in New York?"

"I'm in school." She rolled her eyes towards the ceiling. "And, I can't wait to get that over with and get on with my life."

Mitch grinned. "How much longer do you have?"

"For what I want," Sophia said lifting her shoulders, "it will be a few years."

Mitch said, "That time will pass before you know it, then you'll have all that behind you and you'll be doing your thing."

They didn't notice the ice cream had arrived until it was placed on the table between them. Then they both looked up.

"One banana split with two cherries on top," Angelo, for lack of a name, announced gaily. He had put two spoons in it. Sophia clapped in glee. How could he know she liked banana splits? Angelo looked on in approval, told them to "enjoy" and he went back to cleaning. He began humming to the song as his cloth moved back and forth over the countertop and tables.

"What are your plans when you're out of school?" Mitch asked.

She watched as he grabbed a spoon in his big, sexy hand, scooped some ice cream, pineapples and chocolate sauce up and took it to his waiting mouth. She watched as he put the treat inside, chewed and swallowed. She watched his Adam's apple bob up and down with the movement. *He looked so confident,* Sophia thought.

"I want to be a fashion designer, make fabulous clothes for women all over the world, but my dream is to participate in New York's Fashion Week. That is New York's premier fashion events and to have models strut my clothing up and down that fabulous runway would be major."

Mitch looked over at her. "Make it happen, Sophia. I think you can do anything you set your mind on doing. You appear to have such drive. I don't know you very well but I think you are the kind of girl who will make anything happens that you want. Just go for it!" he exclaimed. "I imagine that one day I will pick up one of my wife's magazine and see some of your fashions in it." Mitch witnessed the look of disappointment on Sophia's face again. Did she think he was single, he wondered. "That wouldn't surprise me at all."

"Thank you for the vote of confidence."

Mitch gave a little laugh. "Oh, no doubt. You certainly are living in the right location; New York City, the fashion capitols of the world."

Sophia looked at Mitch in surprise. "That would be true. Though, I wouldn't think most men would associate with something like that."

"My wife is one of those women who are into what's in and what's not. She loves it all. Clothes, shoes, jewelry…the works."

"And, I'll just bet you make sure that she gets every piece of jewelry or designer shoes and purse that her little heart desires, right?"

"Are you being cynical?"

"Not at all. Just a question."

"I do what I can" Mitch replied.

"I'm sure you do, Mitch." After a moment, Sophia asked, "What about you? What's your story?"

Sophia picked up her spoon while waiting for him to answer and it was Mitch's turn to watch her. He watched as the tip of her small pink tongue snaked out to touch the creamy treat before daintily taking it into her sensuous lips. She made eating ice cream seem so erotic but he couldn't be thinking thoughts like that. He was, after all, married.

"I don't really have much of a story. "I live in Philadelphia, I'm in the real estate business. Right now, I'm trying to make partner. I'm married, we have one son,

Evan, and my wife and I are vacationing here also."

"It'll happen," Sophia said so confidently as if she'd known Mitch for a very long time. "You are intelligent, you represent yourself well and I am sure you know the business so I am willing to bet that you will make partner in, let me see," she paused a moment to think, "I'd say within the next six months to a year."

Mitch chuckled. "That long, huh?"

"Perhaps sooner."

"You really think so?"

"Yes, as a matter of fact, I am certain of it."

Mitch smiled brightly. "From your lips to my bosses' ears." Then, he brought the conversation back to Sophia. "What do you do for fun?

"I hang out with my friends. My two BFFs are Diamond and Afrika. We hang out with Afrika's sister sometimes. She's back at the club also. We go on trips, we go to the clubs, check out hot movies and just do things, you know? I came here on vacation with Africa and her older sister. We came here to get some sun, meet some cute guys and have some good drinks. Diamond is usually with us but she is somewhere in the South of France. Diamond is gangsta. She throws more shade than anyone that I know," Sophia chuckled, showing a lot of pride for her friend. "Diamond is the most gangsta chic that I know and that girl can throw more shade than anyone that I know. That's just how she rolls. She can be one hot mess, but she's my girl."

Mitch threw his head back and laughed. "Gangsta, hot mess, throwing shade, that's how she rolls. You young people are using the weirdest slangs." Mitch shook his head and laughed some more.

Sophia laughed as well. "That's just how we roll," she said, grinning. "Diamond and her family go to the South of France every year and she's already smeared all over Instagram, Facebook, Twitter, she tells me.

Diamond's hobby is to take selfies and put them out there for the world to see." Sophie laughed and Mitch joined in, but he was thinking it appeared they were worlds apart in things that interest them. But, that was that younger generation and the things they were doing, the things Mitch's son, he was certainly, was following and had lots of social media followers, just for the fun of it.

Still laughing, Sophie said, "Diamond lives for that stuff. She is on so many social media sites that it is a miracle that she gets anything of importance done. You'll never believe though that she is a straight A student. Imagine that. She is having great fun, sharing her experiences with the world. The three of us here, man, we give Myrtle Beach a whole new attitude."

Mitch threw his head back, laughing.

CHAPTER 3

Sophia and Mitch continued to laugh easy together. He said, "Apparently she knows what she wants, she stays focused and she gets the job done. Sounds like a remarkable young woman."

"She is that." Sophia glanced over at Mitch. "She and I will compare notes when we get back to the city, because I am having one heck of a great time myself," Sophia chuckled. "Afrika and Diamond are just the best. I don't know what I would do without my peeps. We are all in school and can't wait to be through with that so that we can get involved in our own lives and make some things happen." Sophia's eyes were sparkling with excitement. "Whenever we can, we go out, we get all turnt up and just make it rain in the clubs, man."

"You all make it rain in the clubs, huh?" Mitch laughed some more.

"That's right. Every chance we get," she giggled.

"Isn't that such a vast waste of money, making it rain in the clubs. How often do you ladies do that?"

"Of course it not a waste. It's fun besides, it's not my money. My daddy still supports me so it's really his money. But, anyway, he has a boat load of it and we just have fun with it."

"Are Diamond and Afrika still on their daddy's payrolls also?" Mitch said, finding humor in the fact that all three young ladies were still in school, came from wealthy parents and their parents were still supporting them.

"I would imagine that at some point they will have to cut the umbilical cord, don't you think?" Mitch said laughing.

"You'd think so, but for some reason, most fathers don't want to see their little girls grow up. If fathers could keep us as babies all of our lives, we would never leave the crib."

That caused Mitch to chuckle and Sophia joined in.

After a moment, Mitch said, "I'm under the impression you're a little gangsta yourself."

"Really? Why?"

"I'm of the opinion that you can set a town on fire all by yourself, so if your friends are like minded, well, look out."

Sophia laughed out loud. "I don't know how you know that but it is true. We party hard. Don't get me wrong, we study hard and do what we need to do in school, but we play equally as hard.

"As long as you balance everything, I don't think there's anything wrong with that. All in good honest fun, right?"

"Let me correct that," Sophia said laughing again, "I think we party a little harder than we played, but as you said, it was all good honest fun." Then, she looked unsmilingly at Mitch and asked, "How long have you been married?"

"Right at twenty years."

"Where is your wife tonight?"

"She's out. At least she was when I left the hotel."

Sophia's ears perked up. "You two are on vacation and she's somewhere else without you?"

"Yeah," was Mitch's one word reply.

"Why is that, may I ask?" she inquired out of compassion. "That just seems odd to me."

"It was her decision."

"You didn't want to accompany her?"

If Sophia only knew, Mitch thought, but he had no intention of getting into that.

She continued. "It wouldn't have been your choice to go out separately from her, would it?"

"Honestly, no."

"Is that why you looked so miserable earlier tonight?" She asked with concern.

Mitch looked at her, a puzzled expression on his face. "I look miserable?"

"When you came into the club tonight, I thought you looked miserable, really sad."

Mitch worried that his personal feelings showed to a point that others could see it, but he said, "I don't know why you would say that."

"Because it shows all over your body," she said using her hand to gesture. "Are you saying you're not?"

"I'm fine."

"Liar!"

"You're calling me a liar again. You know that's the second time tonight that you've called me a liar. Why do you insist that I am lying to you?"

"Because you are lying," she answered. Then she shrugged her shoulders and said, "If you say you weren't miserable earlier, then have it your way. That's fine with me"

Mitch inhaled deeply. At that moment, Mitch's phone vibrated in his pants pocket, breaking into his reflections. He wondered whether Kaline was back at the hotel and wanted to know where he was or had she gotten herself into a situation again and needed his help. It'd happened before. Kaline was a beautiful woman and there were times when she would flirt and attract the wrong kind of attention. When she couldn't handle the situation, she would call Mitch to remove the threat.

"Excuse me a second. I need to take this," he said, getting up and walking away from the table, Mitch lifted his phone from his pocket and checked to see who the caller was. Relieved it wasn't Kaline, he answered it.

"Hey man, what's up?" Mitch asked and listened.

"I hope I'm not calling too late and I especially hate calling you while you're on vacation but you did say I could call anytime if I had a problem," Jameson, a co-worker of Mitch's, stated.

"Sure, Jameson. What's going on?"

"Something happened with my computer. The damn thing crashed and I lost all of my listings."

Jameson was a new employee on probation and was reluctant to ask anyone other than Mitch for help. Mitch could hear the uneasiness in his voice. "You need a copy of the listing?" Mitch asked.

"Yeah, man if you don't mind."

"I have that listing. I will shoot Gizelle a text tonight and have her get a copy to you. Oh and Jameson, I have lots of notes on another piece of property. You know the piece over on Gouvener Street."

"I thought you were interested in working that property."

"I've got more than enough to keep me busy. I will get all that to you first thing in the morning."

"Thanks, Mitch. You're the best."

"Everything else is okay?"

"Just more of the same."

"Don't get caught up in the office politics, man. You never know when something will come back and bite you." Mitch thought it was only fair to advise Jameson because the real estate was one of those cut throat businesses where someone was always trying to get ahead by any means necessary, even when it meant lying on someone or throwing them under the bus. Their office wasn't any different.

"I am in your debt, Mitch."

"No problem."

Mitch ended the call and lifted a finger to Sophia and said, "Just give me one more minute please."

Sophie waited patiently eating the delicious dessert while Mitch sent a text to his assistant. Then, he returned his phone to his pocket.

Mitch put his phone back into his pocket and returned to the table. "Now, I'm all yours," he teased as he picked his spoon back up.

"I like the sound of that," Sophia said and they chuckled

As they resumed their treat, Mitch's phone vibrated again. He again lifted his phone from his pocket and after answering a question for his assistant, Mitch put away his phone again.

"Sorry about that," he apologized.

"Can't get away from work, can you?" Sophia glanced up at him. Then, giggling, she thrust her spoon into the mountain of sweet. But, wanting to keep Mitch's undivided attention, Sophia said, "Please let me have your phone."

"Why? What are you going to do with it?" Mitch questioned, dropping his spoon. Then, he went on to explain. "I'm a bit of a workaholic myself, but this kind of thing happens all the time. It's kind of hard to not be involved when you're part of a large firm and so much is going on all the time. We get numerous listings and we're fortunate to still be afloat when so many realty companies are going belly-up." He picked up his spoon to resume eating.

"It's cool that you're a nice guy and extend yourself that way," Sophia began, "but so often, nice guys get taken advantage of. You know what they say, nice guys finish last."

Sophia listened to Mitch as they continued to eat. "Jameson got the job one of our older brokers wanted so it appears that he may be trying to sabotage Jameson's work. He's one of our youngest agents who came to us three months ago. He's smart, hard-working and he's a super nice guy."

"Umm."

Mitch glanced up at the ceiling. "So where were we?" he asked rhetorically but Sophia responded.

"We can be anywhere you want to be," she said, clearly flirting but unsmiling and looking directly into Mitch's eyes.

A surprised Mitch looked at Sophia. Understanding her bold look, he broke into a wide grin and shaking his head, he said, "You are a very funny girl."

"No, I am unflinchingly honest," she replied, giving him her sexiest look.

Mitch chuckled. "You are something else."

"I can be that too," Sophia said with great ease.

Mitch looked at her and they shared a laugh.

"You are a nice man, Mitch Harding. Very sweet, caring." She placed a soft hand on his arm.

"And, how do you know that? Is that your woman's intuition kicking in again," Mitch said, laughing it off.

"I don't know what it is but I am right with most things."

"Ms. Clairvoyant," Mitch teased, and added, "Better keep that quiet otherwise people are gonna have you hanging a sign and starting your own business."

When they stopped laughing, Sophia said, "I like you, Mitch. I like you a lot."

"I like you too, Sophia."

"So, what are we gonna do about it," she said, spiritedly.

Sophia's energy was so infectious it was easy to get caught up in it, but Mitch said, looking at his watch. "I'm gonna walk with you back to where your friends are at the club and then I'm going to my hotel."

Angelo chose that moment to interrupt to tell them that he really needed to close up so he could get home to his wife. They each ate the last bit of ice cream and Mitch picked up one of the cherries by its stem and held it close to Sophia's lips. She rubbed her lips over the cherry before parting them to gently suck the glistening fruit in to slowly chew it. Her eyes never left Mitch's face. Mitch couldn't pull his gaze away and his breath caught in his throat between a groan and a sigh. He shook his head to clear his wayward thoughts before pushing away from the table. She didn't wait for him to come around to help her out of her seat but bounced up and walked to him. They thanked Angelo for his hospitality, Mitch left him a generous tip and they walked out onto the sidewalk.

Once outside, Sophia wrapped her arms around Mitch and squealed, "Oh, no, Mitch. Please," she pleaded, squeezing him to her. "I don't want to go back to that stuffy old club where all those old men were undressing me with their eyes."

"I thought you didn't notice," Mitch chuckled and Sophia joined in.

"Seriously though, Mitch, I don't want the evening to end. Please, let's just stay out here a while longer. Let's take a walk on the beach."

Sophia looked so happy, that Mitch didn't want to deny her that small request. Besides, there was something about her that made him want to learn more about her. "Okay, but just a little while longer."

"Come on." Sophia clapped her hands before impatiently grabbing Mitch's hand to lead him towards the beach.

Mitch hesitated briefly. He didn't want to walk on a beach with someone else other than his wife but he wasn't sure his wife was at the suite waiting for him. As he thought about it, Mitch knew if he went back to his hotel, he'd be in their suite alone because Kanile would be out partying and probably wouldn't return until daybreak as usual.

"Do you always get what you want?"

"Always."

Mitch grinned as he shook his head. "Okay, come on, but just for a little while."

Sophia appeared satisfied with that. She released him, and they continued their walk and engaged in stimulating conversation. Mitch kicked at something in the sand before he bent down to pick up a seashell. He examined it in the moonlight before he brushed it on his pants to remove the remaining sand from it. He looked at the seashell again. "Perfect. This one is gorgeous. Take a look," he said and handed it to Sophia.

She took the seashell from Mitch's hand and exclaimed happily, "Oooooh, this is beautiful." Sophia carefully examined their find and it was perfect, not a crack or chip in it, and she turned her excited dancing eyes to Mitch, "This is mine, right. May I have it, please? I simply cannot give this back. I love it. Please, please, may I keep it?"

"You certainly may. You will probably get rid of it before you leave Myrtle Beach," Mitch said, smiling down at her.

"I am going to keep it forever," she replied, holding the item in her hand and putting it up to her heart.

"So, if you and I happen to run into each other, say, fifty years from now, you will still have the shell, right?"

"Absolutely. I will treasure it for the rest of my life."

"Yeah, sure," Mitch said, going along with what she'd said whether he believed her or not.

The light of the moon embraced the ocean and caressed Mitch and Sophia, and the silky sand squish between their toes as they strolled bare footed along the beach. Mitch stared down at their joined hands, then he looked out across the water. When he looked back at Sophia, he wasn't thinking about his harpy wife or his extravagant bills. He was thinking about this woman who was so vibrant, so alluring, so drop dead gorgeous. Sophia was so damn hot. Mitch didn't know what had gotten into him. He had a good marriage, for the most part, and he was very much in love with his wife. There was no doubting that. There were even times when Mitch believed Kaline was in love with him. With that in mind, he had to wonder why he was walking on the beach, holding hands with this gorgeous stranger, and feeling so comfortable. What the hell was that about? He was behaving like some horny school boy or worst, a damn lunatic going through mid-life crisis. But, this was the best he'd felt all week. In fact, this was the best he had felt in quite a while.

"Heavenly," she said, echoing his thoughts. He gave her a questioning look. Digging her feet in the moist sand and looking up at the moon lit sky; she pushed back hair from her face and said, "It's a beautiful night."

"Yes it is," he agreed, but his agreement was more about her beauty than the night.

At this time of night the beach was practically deserted, only an occasional couple wandered by. Sophia abruptly turned to Mitch, moving closely to him, pressing her body against his. She felt his breath as it fanned her face. Excitement seeped into her, heat was winding through the pit of her stomach.

Her nearness was playing tricks on Mitch's senses. He could have moved, he should have moved, but he didn't. Why didn't he move away from her? The thought was running around inside Mitch's head when, suddenly and boldly Sophia reached down and took his member into her hand.

Mitch didn't know how much Sophia had to drink before they met tonight or whether it was the alcohol that was causing her to behave this way but he was taken aback by what she had done and it took a moment for him to respond. He quickly jerked his member out of her reach and caught her hand restricting it but not quickly enough to prevent his penis from leaping with awareness to her touch. His member had already come alive and grew harder and larger by the second.

"What are you doing, young lady?" he asked, almost as shocked by her action as he was about the response of his own body.

"I'm enjoying myself," she replied, smiling and looking unashamedly into his eyes.

"Has anyone ever told you that you are a bad girl? A very bad girl." He gave her the kind of look an adult would give to a child who was misbehaving.

"No, actually I have never been called a bad girl, but there's something to be said about that."

Mitch was confused. He asked, "about being called a bad girl?"

"A very bad girl," she corrected, giggling. Then, suddenly she became serious. "Don't get it twisted, Mitch. I have never approached anyone the way I have you."

"Are you sure about that?" he asked, thinking that as forward as this young woman was, she probably had plenty experience with other men.

"Why would I lie to you?" Her question was almost nonchalant. "There is something about you that caused me to act that way. Being with you causes me to lose my head."

Shaking his head in disbelief, Mitch resumed walking and said, "You don't really expect me to believe that, do you?"

Sophia didn't care whether Mitch believed her or not, she just wanted to touch his thick, heavy member again. She had already decided to do it and that's all there was to it. She just had to. She wanted to feel his manhood in her hand, hold him in her hand, stroke him and enjoy the way he responded to her touch. And, and the look she gave him told him as much. With him, she felt so liberated, like some untamed beast, grabbing and taking what she wanted without consent or apology, and it felt good. "I don't care what you think. I happen to know that it's true. I don't normally behave this way with anyone but as I said, there is something about you that causes me to

behave this way. You are different, Mitch.
You are a gorgeous man, you've got a hot
body and that appeals to everything in me."

"Oh, really?" Mitch felt an alarm bell go
off inside his head that went all the way
down his spine and ending in a jolt at his
feet. He was a flesh and blood man with as
much sexual drive as any man. How much
of this could he take? How much could he
be expected to take? Though he was
flattered by all the attention she was laying
on him, at the same time, he knew this
situation was heading into dangerous waters.

"Yes really," she replied, twirling around
him playfully. Then she added, "I feel so
uninhibited, so unrestricted out here with
you." Her eyes danced with excitement.

Mitch smiled back at her before he asked,
"I just don't get it. I mean, wouldn't you
rather be out here walking along this nearly
deserted beach on this absolutely beautiful
night with someone more your own age,
someone who has more in common with
you?" He gave her a polite look.

"You really do have a problem with the age thing, don't you? Why does that bother you so much, Mitch? I don't have a problem with your age." Before Mitch could speak, Sophia said, "Guys my age act so childish and silly, they make me laugh. I don't really have much in common with guys my age."

"And how old is that?"

"Don't you know a woman never tells her age?"

"It really doesn't matter," he lied. "I was just wondering."

As Sophia looked at Mitch, all she could think about was that Mitch's strong, masculine and chiseled, brown skinned face and body reminded her of a black version of the handsome Marlboro Man whose image used to be plastered on large billboards around the country. Mitch exuded a thoughtless kind of sensuality.

Although Sophia was five feet, eight, Mitch was at least six two with everything hard in the right places and that nice six pack he was sporting was a delicious bonus. He boasted of a generous head of dark hair, a perfect nose, and there was absolutely nothing wrong with his full luscious lips. But, what struck Sophia most about Mitch were his eyes. The warm, wide set, mesmerizing, sexy as hell, hazel eye were catlike, hypnotizing and were the most gorgeous eyes Sophia had ever seen. If she could have made love to Mitch's eyes, the pleasure would have been hers. She would have done so in a heartbeat.

Sophia knew Mitch was older than she and even if he hadn't told her, she would have guessed that he was married. Men like Mitch would not have escaped some woman snatching him up and making him her own. He looked like the kind of man who didn't have any trouble getting his fair share of women in his day or even today, for that matter. But Sophia didn't care. *Every woman for herself*, she thought.

"I am old enough," she answered, smiling sexily at him. "I am a woman and I know what I want. That makes me old enough, doesn't it?"

Sophia turned to look at him as they continued to walk. "How old do you want me to be?"

"I don't know," he chuckled. "Thirty-five, forty maybe," he teased.

Sophia laughed. "Well, I am not forty or even thirty-five, at least not yet, but age is not important. It ain't nothing but a number. You remember," she said and she began to sing the lyrics to Aaliyah's song that she was referencing. She moved her feet in a dance move and snapped her fingers to the tune.

"Yeah, I know the song."

"Well, that should stop you being concerned about my age and you being an old man. It's boring and I don't want to hear it." Her fierceness caught him off guard. His eyes grew wide. In a gentler voice she added, "Mitch, I'm attracted to you and that's easy. I look at you and I like what I see." She lifted a hand and touched the side of his face. "You are kind, you are thoughtful and you are funny in a good way. You and I enjoy each other's company. What's not to like? You are enjoying my company, aren't you?"

"Yes, very much," he had to admit. His hazel eyes gleamed at her.

"Then, what's the problem?" She sounded exasperated.

"I didn't say there was a problem," he said, but the heat and the feel of her body against his when they danced was etched in his memory, and she was causing the same kind of sensation now so whether he wanted to admit it or not, that was a Problem—with a capital P.

"But you're acting like it is and I don't know why you feel that way. We're not hurting anyone," she said and walked off ahead of him. Then suddenly she turned, looked at him, her eyes holding his. "Do you want to make love to me, Mitch?"

He didn't respond—couldn't respond. Again he was taken aback by Sophia's boldness. He didn't know whether he should be flattered and attracted by this young woman's behavior or run like hell away from it.

Interrupting his thoughts, Sophia's beautiful mouth was unsmiling when she asked, "Well, do you?" Her mouth formed a perfect circle on the words, 'do' and 'you.'

He shook his head, "no," but his eyes told a different story, and she told him so.

"That's not what I hear in your voice. It's what I feel in my heart, what I know in my soul but more importantly, it's what I see in your eyes and the eyes are the window to our soul. Your eyes are telling an entirely different story."

He took his eyes from hers. He decided that might be best because one more look into those beautiful dark sexy pools that stared back at him may become one look too many. Mitch asked, "Are you serious right now?" He tried to act casual, as if what she'd said was far from the truth. Sophia stood back and silently watched him, a telltale look on his face. "What?" he asked, feeling a little uncomfortable.

"You do want to have sex with me."

"No," he replied almost too quickly that time. Hell, he was damned if he did or damned if he didn't.

"You're lying," she accused with ease and confidence. "Not only do your eyes betray you but you can't even trust my friend down below either," she said, indicating Mitch's penis as she giggled.

Mitch didn't speak. All he could do was shake his head. He had met a lot of women in his time but none quite like Sophia. She was bolder than anyone he had seen in a while. "You can admit it," she continued. "I won't tell anyone. Besides," she looked around in a sweeping gesture, toying with him or rather torturing him… and enjoying it, "there's no one around for me to tell, so you see, your secret is safe with me."

"I told you, Sophia, I'm a married man and even if, for some crazy reason I did want to make love to you, I couldn't or more to the point, I just wouldn't."

"Why?"

Mitch looked at Sophia a moment, then without answering her question, he said, "you are a gorgeous girl and I'm sure you've got lots of guys lined up, wanting to be with you."

"And?"

"I'm just saying."

"I'm very selective, and I hadn't found what I've been looking for until now. I know what I want, Mitch." She stared into his eyes and with a sinful smile plastered across her face said, "And, so do you. It's in your eyes."

"Either you've had too much to drink," Mitch said in good humor, "or you have a dirty little mind." He trying to play it off, but the intense desire reflecting in his eyes revealed the truth, causing her spirits to soar.

Her body dangerously close to his again, she said, "Liar," and pressed her body hard against his before she walked away from him, giggling.

"You really are flirting with me, aren't you?" He grinned, continuing to make light of their conversation as he followed her.

"Absolutely," she said casually, with an exaggerated wiggle of her shapely hips. She was like a modern day Eve tempting Adam with flesh on a body that was pure perfection—captivating. "Our body language always gives us away, you know. We could very easily allow our bodies to finish our conversation. I know you want that just as much as I do, but you would feel guilty and think you were a terrible man if you admitted it. That's the kind of man you are," she hesitated a moment before walking away and over her shoulder, she finished her statement, "I think."

Mitch caught up with her, took her by her arm and turned her so that she could face him. "Look Sophia, it's not that I don't find you attractive because I do. I've been saying all night that you are one gorgeous woman, but I am married. My wife and I are here on vacation. In another few days we will be going back to our lives in Philadelphia and you and I will probably never see each other again….."

Sophia interrupted him saying, "I am not asking you to marry me."

"I'm not sure what you are asking of me," Mitch grinned. "What is it that you think you want from me?"

"Do I have to spell it out?"

Mitch gazed into her eyes, giving her a knowing look. "Let's be serious. We both know that ain't gonna happen."

Without wavering, she returned his gaze. "Are you happy, Mitch?"

"Yeah," he released her shoulders and stuffed his hands into his pockets. "Reasonably so but who's happy all the time?"

"What do you want most in life?"

He looked at her a moment before he responded. "That's easy," he began. "I'd like a grandchild or two, be able to take care of my family the way they deserve to be, and live a long, healthy and happy life."

"It doesn't take much to make you happy."

"No, it really doesn't. I'm a rather simple man."

"I don't agree with that."

"No?"

"Of course now."

"You have your own opinion, Ms. Clairvoyant."

"Are you laughing at me?"

"Not really," he said and asked, "and what is your heart's desire?"

Sophia's voice became very soft and her eyes began to dream when she said, "I like living my life. I don't want to live in a bubble or conform to anyone else's standards or rules. I don't want life to just pass me by. I want to feel it as I live it. I have just got to feel things. You know what I mean?"

Mitch thought for a moment. That was exactly how he would prefer to live his life, only that wasn't how it had turned out, but he said, "Yes, I do. I know exactly what you mean."

As time passed, Sophia found she was attracted to Mitch and it seemed perfectly natural to her. "If I could have anything I want, it would be you," she replied matter of fact.

Mitch's head snapped in her direction. "What?" He was incredulous. "That is insane," he said, shaking his head, humor glinting in his eyes.

"Not really. I just know that I want you. I have everything else."

Mitch gave a little chuckle. "Are you always so sure about what you want?"

"Yes, I am."

"That could get you into a lot of trouble."

"Now that you have sufficiently warned me, what are you going to do with that?"

He pulled his hands out of his pockets. He reached down and picked up another seashell that he examined before tossing it back into the ocean after noting its flaws.

"Not a thing, little momma," as he lapsed into silence.

In the quiet that ensued, Sophia shared that she was an only child to wealthy, society, country club type parents who would commit suicide or have Mitch killed if they knew he was walking on the beach with their precious daughter.

"Then we, or should I say *I* had better not get caught," Mitch quipped which lightened the mood.

Sophia dropped her stilettos and purse in the sand. Then, she reached her arms up around Mitch's neck. "I do want you, Mitch, and I want you now!"

Her gaze flickered over his mouth. Then, a terrible urgency gripped her, pushing her to go after what she wanted, and what she wanted was to discover more about this man; his taste, his weak spot, what excited him more than the next breath he knew he had to take. Everything! At that moment, she felt an overwhelming desire to taste his well-shaped, sensual lips. She stared into his eyes and pulled him down, wanting to feel his lips on hers, wanting his kiss more than she had wanted anything in her life before. Without further pause, her tongue slid over his lips a moment before she quickly pushed it into his mouth. Initially, his hands went to her shoulders to restrain her, but she held him tighter.

As she kissed him, she did so with a gentleness and restraint he couldn't deny. Just as he couldn't deny how much he liked the taste of the kiss and the feel of her soft, sexy body pressing against his, Mitch knew he shouldn't be allowing this to happen or having those kinds of feelings but he couldn't resist sliding his arms from her shoulders down to her slender waist and pulling her closer to him as he kissed her back. Their first kiss came as a surprise to Mitch but not Sophia. She'd known from the time they stepped out of that club together that this kiss was inevitable. She was just trying to give him the opportunity to realize it as well.

Melting into his strong embrace, her kiss became passionate and womanly. It was everything a kiss should be—urgent, seeking, satisfying and yet curiously unsatisfying, all at the same time, leaving each of them wanting more—much more.

As Mitch began to enjoy the kiss, a pierce of longing so sharp shot through him that it hurt. Suddenly, Sophia tore away from him. She pulled her dress over her head and after tossing it on the ground near her shoes and purse, she ran towards the ocean. At first, she just kicked her feet in the water at the edge. Then quickly, she started advancing deeper into the ocean— the water around her waist now.

A surprised Mitch yelled, "What are you doing, Sophia? Where are you going?"

She responded with a giggle. Before Mitch realized, he'd kicked off his shoes, ran into the ocean and was wading in the water after her. When he caught up to her, she immediately jumped into his arms. Without hesitation, she wrapped her arms tightly around his neck and her legs around his waist and she began kissing him again. This kiss was even more passionate, more intense. He should be breaking speed limits getting away from Sophia but here he was joining her in making the situation worst.

Mitch sucked her lips, her tongue with such force, that he thought he heard her whimper, trying to cry out. He allowed his tongue to play with hers, to tease it as he rotated his tongue around hers before pulling all of it into his mouth and sucked hard on it until she tore her mouth away to catch a breath.

His mouth brushed her beautiful porcelain cheek. Then he ventured down her neck, kissing and nibbling the soft, delicate skin and finally his mouth returned to hers. He kissed her again and again until the tightening in his groin made him sick. This time, it was Mitch who ended the kiss. He swore silently as he pushed away from her. It took every ounce of strength within him to put a stop to this, but he had to. He simply had to.

"What's wrong?" she giggled.

"Sophia, this isn't funny. We're crossing the line on a number of levels and you know that."

"And we haven't even had sex yet."

Mitch sighed, threw his hands in the air. He felt he had humored Sophia but this had gone on far enough. He decided it was time to go. Get the hell out of Dodge. He definitely had to get away from Sophia because his flesh wanted to do so much more to her flesh than he had a right to do.

Interrupting Mitch's thoughts, Sophia said, "It's beautiful how the moon magically dips down and embraces the ocean, creating a silvery path across the water as far as the eyes can see. It's as though we can walk across the ocean and go straight up to the moon. It really is magical," Sophia said, lifting her head to the sky and wrapping her arms around her middle. "Magic is all around us. All we have to do is look closely and it's there."

Mitch was pleased with Sophia's energy but he was impressed by her intelligence. He trained his eyes in the direction as Sophia's and instead of giving her a quick, flippant answer, he surprised himself again when he said, "There're so many things that we question about what goes on around us. But in the end, we know that they all are God's gifts for us to live by, learn from or to simply enjoy."

"Aaah, that's sweet," she said, a dreamy look on her face. "It appears you have some romantic bones in that magnificent body of yours after all."

Mitch shrugged his broad shoulders and scratched his head. "I suppose to some extent, most of us do."

After wading in the water a while, Mitch and Sophia walked out of the ocean together, he picked up her dress and shoes from the ground and handed them to her. Instead of taking the dress from his extended hand, Sophia raised both hands over her head so that he could help her get into it. Mitch held Sophia's shoes between his thighs and lifted her dress over her head and it settled in place on her body.

"Do you want me to see you back to the club or your hotel?"

For a single second Sophia appeared disappointed. "Must we end the evening so soon?"

Mitch was sorry to have caused her sadness, but he gave her a stern look and answered, "Yes, we really do."

Sophia made a face. "Well, if we must, would you please walk with me to my hotel?"

"Sure I will. Are you staying nearby?"

"Look, I wasn't trying to make you feel bad or rejected because that definitely wasn't my intention. Sophia, you should never feel rejected by anyone. You really are that special."

Then her quick, beautiful smile was back and as bewitching as ever. "Thank you and yes, I am staying nearby. Are you going to spend the night with me?"

"You've got to be kidding," Mitch said, looking at her. When the look Sophia gave him told him she wasn't kidding, he said, "No, I'm not spending the night with you, but I will see that you get to your hotel safely."

For Mitch, safety had absolutely nothing to do with any physical harm coming upon Sophia. He was more concerned with his own. It was a beautiful night. The moon was full and the surf rolled in and out splashing against their ankles.

Sophia responded by reaching over and catching Mitch's hand. He didn't pull his hand away. She entwined her fingers with his. Then she looked down at his long and narrow hand with tapering fingers. She lifted her eyes to him again before turning away. There, with their feet planted in the sand, they watched the moon edge its way across the sky marking the judgment of time. There, the comfort they suddenly felt made disclosing their personal histories easy, almost natural.

As they made their way back down the beach, Mitch shared with Sophia how miserable the past couple of days had been. "You are so easy to talk to," he said to Sophia but wished he could say the same about his wife. How could he tell anyone that his wife didn't agree with anything he said and found something wrong with everything he did?

"She doesn't support your choices?" Sophia wanted to know. It was as if she had read his mind.

"I don't have any choices as far as she is concerned," he replied, his eyes had narrowed, his voice had lowered, and he had spoken with a hint of bitterness, giving Sophia the oddest feeling that there were major problems in his marriage.

"That is terrible." Sophia touched his shoulder. "Why do you allow her to treat you that way?" When Mitch didn't answer, she said, "I can tell you care a great deal about your wife and you want the very best for her but you appear to be conflicted. Caring about someone shouldn't be a struggle. It should be fun, loving, enjoyable." Sophia looked up briefly at Mitch before asking, "Why do you stay with her? Seriously, Mitch, life is short; it is measured in moments so we have to take advantage of each moment. If your wife doesn't treat you like the man you are and she doesn't make you happy, you shouldn't be there."

Wow, that's bold, Mitch thought and he answered her honestly. "Because I love her."

"How is that working for you?" Sophia said, kicking the sand. "Does she love you?"

Mitch's handsome face grimaced. This young lady was really stepping way out of her lane with those kinds of questions, but he answered. "Yes, she does," he said, then rephrased his response, "At least I think she does. She loves me the man but she doesn't have much respect for where I am in life," he said, suddenly looking uncomfortable.

"Can you really separate the two?" Sophia asked thoughtfully, turning her head to one side.

Mitch shook his head, looking down at his feet as the waves twirled around his ankles. "I really don't know anymore," he answered honestly with a deep sigh.

"You shouldn't be going through that crap. You should be living each day as if it were your last. Life should be exciting, stimulating otherwise we are simply existing. Just marking time." She punched him in the arm. "That's what I do. I have fun and I don't think about the consequences."

Mitch looked up at Sophia with a half-smile and said, "Hah! Don't you think that's a bit irresponsible?"

"It is if you merely want to exist," she answered. "You have to go out there and live hard; live strong before life passes you by. Just do it."

Mitch snickered. "What are you? A Nike spokesperson?"

Sophia chuckled. Then, she looked thoughtful for a moment before asking, "Have you ever heard the expression, sometimes you have to step apart from something before you come apart?"

"Are you talking about me?"

"Would you answer the question, please?"

Mitch stroked his chin. "No, I don't think I ever have, but I understand its meaning."

"My dad used to use that expression all the time and it used to drive my mom crazy. It wasn't even meant for her, but she hated it." Sophia said, then, seeing the dejected look on Mitch's face, she added, assuring him in a lighthearted manner, "I could fix your pained situation."

Before Mitch could respond, Sophia removed the diamond encrusted comb from her hair and dropped it into her purse. As the breezes picked up and washed over her, waking up her skin, she shifted her long, thin fingers through her hair, allowing the silk, copper tresses to cascade below her shoulders.

After weighing his question a moment, Mitch asked, "Would I be getting all up in your business if I said it's obvious that you are not here with anyone special?"

"Is that obvious to you?"

"Would you be out partying without a date, then come out here with me if you were here with a significant other?"

The moment the words escaped Mitch's lips, he was sorry because that's exactly what was happening with he and his wife, he thought, and Sophia's thoughts matched his exactly but she didn't say anything.

Just then, they were fortunate enough to see a falling star and Sophia didn't let the opportunity to make a wish, escape. "Oh look!" she exclaimed, excitedly, pointing toward the star. She put her hands up to her mouth and closed her eyes for a brief moment.

When Sophia opened her eyes again, Mitch asked, "What did you wish for?"
"I can't tell you."

"Why not?"

"Because if I tell you, my wish won't come true."

Mitch chuckled. "Do you really believe that?"

"Yes, of course I do, but I can tell that you don't."

"No, I don't."

"Why?"

"Because it's silly."

"It is not."

"Are you telling me you believe that if you make a wish upon a falling star that your wish will come true?"

"That's exactly what I'm saying. You don't have to believe it, but tonight is still young and," she glanced up at him with a cunning look, "only time will tell."

Mitch studied her for a moment. Sophia wasn't intimidated about invading his privacy and she was bolder than anyone he had ever met but it felt good sharing with someone who cared about his interests rather than being critical of him. Thinking about how unselfish and caring the young, carefree Sophia was caused Mitch's smile to return not only to his lips but his eyes. He thought how perfect it would have been if only it had been Kanile and not Sophia on the beach, talking and sharing with him.

Suddenly it began to drizzle but Sophia was so cheerful and full of live, she made Mitch forget they were getting wet. For the right man, Sophia could make him feel he could conquer the world.

Mitch rolled his eyes up towards the sky. "I'm over it already. Come on," he said. "It's late. Let's get you to your hotel."

Sophia pouted but she held onto his arm while he slipped her four inch stilettos on her feet, then she caught his hand and almost completely wet, walked with him to her hotel.

Once when Mitch and Kaline went to Myrtle Beach at a business conference, they had stayed at the upscale Ocean Camellia

Resorts where Sophia was staying. The hotel housed an onsite restaurant, a trendy rooftop lounge and glass enclosed pools. Sophia had told Mitch that her father was still supporting her. Well, if the rest of her lifestyle was based on her vacation accommodations at that hotel, she was being supported in grand style.

"What line of work is your father in?" Mitch wanted to know.

"My dad is the owner and CEO of Hartford Construction Company."

Mitch's eyes popped wide open in surprise. "Ah. Hartford Construction Company?"

"Yeah. You know the company?"

"Yes I do, along with everyone else," Mitch teased. "You are that Sophia Hartford?"

"Your father's company is responsible for a lot of the nice architecture around the country."

Sophia smiled up at him.

"Yeah, we are pretty major," she teased and that comment surprised Mitch.

Mitch and Sophia entered the elegant lobby of the Ocean Camellia Resorts Hotel and walked across the marble floor to the elevator. They waited a moment for an elevator to arrive and when one did, they entered and Mitch looked at Sophia and asked, "Which floor?"

"Twelfth," she replied.

He pressed the elevator button denoting the floor where they were going. "Here we go," Mitch said and they moved to the back of the elevator to allow two other couples to enter; one couple who appeared to be middle aged while the other was an elderly couple. They all glanced at Mitch and Sophia and smiled, but the female's eyes of the older couple darted from Sophia to Mitch's face and back again. The older woman's stares didn't cause a problem for Sophia but those stares made Mitch feel a little ashamed. He believed the woman was thinking what he probably would be thinking himself especially if he had a daughter who was in an elevator with a man twice her age that hour of the morning. What is that old fool doing with that young girl?

The elevator came to a stop on the Fourth Floor and the older couple got off but not before the woman gave Mitch and Sophia one final look. The other couple exited the elevator when it stopped on the Fifth Floor, after saying goodbye to Mitch and Sophia. As soon as the elevator doors were closed, Sophia marched up to the front of the elevator, she pressed the STOP button on the wall in the elevator, then she turned to face Mitch, giving him that naughty look he had come to recognize from her.

"You are so bad." He grinned down at her.

Unsmiling, she looked at him and said, "I know. You told me. You won't admit it, but you like it."

"What?" Mitch frowned at her and shaking his head, he said, "You are truly unbelievable."

"Yeah, I know," she looked at him wickedly and in another moment, she quickly moved into his arms. Grateful he didn't try to stop her, instead, his hands slid down her back and he gathered her into his arms. She wrapped her arms around his neck and she began kissing him. She pushed her tongue deep into his mouth and he sucked hungrily on it. Their kiss went from zero to passionate in less than sixty seconds.

Mitch lifted her from the floor and pushed her back against the wall of the elevator as he kissed her. When Sophia's feet were on the elevator floor again, she lifted one leg so that he could touch her intimate part, encouraged him to touch her intimate part as he ground his body hard against hers. Mitch ran his fingers through her long, silky locks. He broke the kiss and looked down into her eyes. In the next second, he gripped her hair with both hands and kissed her, sucking her mouth, her tongue into his mouth in the most primal, savage way. He kissed her with all the pent up emotions he had carried around for much too long. He was certain he felt the earth move. For a moment, for Mitch, time stood still. Sophia thought being with Mitch was like being on drugs and for her, he definitely was her drug of choice.

Mitch and Sophia were hungry for each other; hungry for each other's touch, each other's kiss and as their kiss continued, not only did Sophia's senses reel but her knees weakened and began to buckle. Mitch tightened his grip on her and she clung to him as their kiss grew deeper. They were in a place where magic lives. That was exactly where Sophia wanted to be and she wanted to remain in that sweet place, forever.

Mitch quickened his movements, grounding ferociously against Sophia, with her young tender body pressing tightly against his, answering his every move. Their movements against each other were animalistic. After a while, Mitch broke the kiss, suddenly finding the good sense within himself and realizing they were both running out of control.

Sophia's voice cracked when she asked, "Why did you stop?"

"It's been a great evening, Sophia," Mitch's voice hinted of some emotion. "I've had a great time with you tonight."

Sophia looked at him a long moment before she relented and said, "Okay. If you say so." Then she walked over and hit the button to release the elevator and the button for the Twelfth Floor again. She walked back over to Mitch. With her feet in her four inch stilettos, it was easy to lean in and comfortably rest her head against his chest as they rode together up to the designated floor.

When Mitch and Sophia stood just outside her hotel room door, he looked down at her long, beautiful manicured hands that were holding onto his hand. She was smart, bubbly and sexy, and Mitch hated to leave her yet what choice did he have. "It was fun tonight. I had a great time," he said.

"Would you like to come inside and have a quick drink with me?" she asked, using her keycard to open her room door.

He gave a little laugh. "I don't think so."

"Are you sure?" She batted her eyelashes at him as she tugged his arm again, in a way that reminded him of a little girl. "I won't bite…unless you want me to." She giggled.

"No, it's late. I really have to go."

Mitch caught her petite hands, lifted them to his lips and gently kissed them.
"I had a really good time tonight, Sophia. Thank you so much.
"

"You don't have to thank me, Mitch. I enjoyed spending time with you and getting to know you as well." Then, looking innocently at him, she asked softly, "Will I see you again?"

"I don't think so. Good night." He released her hands and turned to leave.

As Sophia's heart burned for all that Mitch had been through with his wife, she said, "Mitch. He turned to look at her. "Don't allow anyone to change the person you are. You are a really good man; caring, generous, extremely passionate about the people in your life. You are a man who knows who he is and exactly what he wants. You just have to own it, demand that others respect you for who you know you are." Sophia hesitated a moment.

Mitch said, "Don't stop now."

They chuckled together.

"Own who you are. Walk into your life with open arms. You may just get something you didn't expect."

With a small grin on his face, Mitch said, "Are you a philosopher now?"

"No. I am just a student of human behavior."

Although touched by her remarks, Mitch smiled and continued to make light of the situation. "Thank you for the session, doctor. I'll see you again next week."

They laughed again

"I am serious."

"You're sweet. Thank you for that." He kissed her on her forehead and as soon as she cleared the threshold, Mitch closed the door, putting a barrier between them. With Sophia out of reach, Mitch stood with his back against the wall and ran a hand over his head and thought what a man could do with a woman like Sophia by his side. Then, he left.

He walked the short distance back to his hotel with lovely thoughts of Sophia playing around in his mind. He felt so different from the beaten man who had left his suite several hours earlier. Sophia had made him feel so much better. She made him feel so much. More to the point, she made him feel.

It was odd that he was thinking that with someone as supportive and caring as Sophia, he could do anything. She had forced him to look inward and see himself through her eyes and value his own self-worth. Why had he allowed Kaline to speak to him and treat him in such a low degrading manner for longer than he cared to remember? He didn't know why he had allowed it to happen, but now, with Sophia's words ringing in his ear, he knew he would no longer tolerate that behavior from anyone ever again.

As Mitch opened the door to the suite, his thought was that Sophia was going to make some young man very happy one day. He laughed, shook his head and dismissed the young and beautiful Sophia from his mind forever, failing to remember that forever is a very long time.

CHAPTER 4

It was a little after two in the morning when Mitch entered their suite. Kaline wasn't there and it didn't appear she had returned while he was out. Irritated, he removed his clothes, kicked off his shoes sending one across the room hitting the wall with a thud and wondered where his wife was. Mitch dropped down on the side of the bed and smoked a cigarette. Then, he took a long cold shower before going to bed. Exhausted yet unable to sleep, Mitch tossed and turned and watched the face of the clock on the nightstand next to the bed. Where could Kaline be at this hour again? Mitch's anger and suspicion peaked and still unable to sleep, in a huff, he threw back the covers, sprung out of bed and he got dressed. Mitch poured himself a drink that he put down in one huge gulp. Then he had another before leaving their hotel suite and headed to the beach for a late night walk—alone. The night was still beautiful; warm and clear, with stars sparkling in the night sky. He loved the sound of the ocean crashing against the shore. It was a night for lovers and Mitch wished his wife was there to enjoy it with him.

Fifteen minutes later Mitch stood at Sophia's room door. He wasn't sure what brought him there but there were a thousand reasons inside his mind telling him he shouldn't be and a million more reasons telling him to go back to his hotel before it was too late. But it was already too late because Sophia had already flung opened the door. Seeing Mitch there, Sophia shrugged the white night gown off her shoulders and let it slide to the floor at her feet. There she stood, wearing only a sheer white sleeveless pajama top and matching panties made of lace and a lot of promise. Mitch's jaw dropped open and his eyes feverishly traveled the length of Sophia's body several times, taking in everything from her damp hair held atop her head with a white ribbon, down her curvy, magnificent body to her petite bare feet, before his eyes returned to rest on her beautiful face where he admired each feature. The moment Mitch crossed the threshold, each knew something extraordinary was going to happen.

Sophia's sleepwear was revealing much more than Mitch should see or had any right to see. Heat flowed through Mitch's veins. He didn't know where this animal desire for Sophia came from so quickly, so demanding. Mitch knew it was wrong to be there but he was powerless to stop himself. His desire for Sophia was far greater now than any sense of reasoning. He cursed Sophia for getting to him like that, but he cursed himself more for letting her get to him. Sophia was beautiful, energetic, sexy and she had this amazing ability to still

Mitch's mind while simultaneously stirred his senses. The room was alive with electricity. Eagerness, anticipation, stirred the air. Mitch wanted Sophia! Regardless of the consequences, he had to have her!

As he looked at Sophia, Mitch wanted to touch her. Everywhere! All at the same time. And, as if she read his mind, like a tropical storm, she flew into his arms. Mitch pulled Sophia roughly to him, encircled her body in his arms and he held her tightly to him. She willingly melted into his arms, a thrill racing through her body as she focused on bringing air in and out of her lungs. Mitch traced Sophia's jaw line and ran his fingers over her cheekbones. He had never seen anyone so beautiful and she felt so good wrapped in his arms—too good to let her go. As Sophia pressed her body against Mitch, his mouth took hers in a kiss that was, intoxicating, mind blowing, everything he could have hoped for and at that moment, time stood still for Mitch.

They caressed and clawed at each other with Mitch's hands roaming over Sophia's body, fully appreciated her softness, her curves. Sophia's skin was smooth and warm to his touch. Mitch broke the kiss. Sophia's dark, sparkling eyes held his, capturing them as her hands began to tear his shirt from his body.

Mitch began to mutter, "This isn't right. I shouldn't be doing th…" but Sophia's lips interrupted his words and then his thoughts. Devouring each other in the kiss, drinking in its sweetness, they stumbled backward and fell together against the dresser, knocking everything in their path to the floor. Sophia wrapped her arms tightly around Mitch's neck, molding herself to him and using her tongue to trace over his lips before pushing her tongue into his mouth, then deeper into his mouth and he sucked on it trying to take more of it in. As their locked lips fanned their desire, a shudder of desire raced through Mitch as Sophia was inflamed by the sensuous movement of his hips as he ground between her opened legs. She kissed him passionately with total reckless abandon. Her kisses were dangerous and Mitch welcomed them, encouraged them, demand them with his own passion that he didn't recognize.

Mitch tore his mouth from hers and unhooked the single button holding her top together. His eyes moved from hers to her breasts that were high, round globes of perfection. Sophia gasped when Mitch's palms rolled over her nipples. She groaned when he took both nipples between his thumb and forefinger and played with them until they throbbed and burned with indescribable pleasure. Then, Mitch's mouth latched onto one of her breasts and he began suck on it for a while before advancing to the next. Feeling her nipples harden under his mouth, there was no place in his mind for a single rational thought. His only thought was to have Sophia. He had never experienced feelings as raw, strong, powerful as what he was feeling. He wanted more and right or wrong, he had to have more.

With her arms still wrapped around his neck and her legs circling around his waist, in one quick moment, Mitch effortlessly lifted Sophia from the dresser and with her head nestled against his chest, he carried her over to the bed. He slipped his tongue in and out of her mouth explored it some more, luring her tongue to follow. When the connection was made, Mitch was merciless, relentless as his mouth assaulted hers. His strong hands took possession of her firm ripe breasts again and gently squeezed and massaged them before his hands moved down her body and slid under her round hips, cradling them in his palms, bringing her roughly against him. Their lips came apart as he brought her down on the bed atop him, and looking deeply into her eyes, he watched her move down his body.

Without taking her eyes from his, Sophia unzipped Mitch's pants and as he raised his hips for her to push them down his legs, she noticed that he was not wearing underwear. When she saw his engorged member, all she could think was how much she wanted to feel the length of his member inside her. She wanted to own it, even if just for that one night. Sophia took his member into her small hand and began stroking it. Her touch seemed to burn pure fire on his skin. How exciting it had been to bring him to life again in such a stunningly intimate way. She moved down on Mitch, planting kisses on his body along the way, and she heard his gasp when her warm mouth closed on him. Mitch felt helpless as Sophia's mouth and tongue did the most incredible things to him. All he could do was lie there while she tortured and pleasured him all at the same time. When Sophia moved up to straddle Mitch, he pulled her closely and kissed her again and again, taking her breath away as he pushed her panties down her legs and tossed them aside. Mitch had to take a moment to drink in the sight of Sophia's perfect, naked body. He became spellbound. Mitch's eyes returned to her nipples. He sucked and nibbled one nipple, then the next, then as he used his tongue to assault the hard pebbles, Sophia began to moan and thrash her head from side to side, enjoying the sweet punishment he unleashed on her.

Mitch was dazed as he sucked and nibbled Sophia's breast. The only reality to him now was that Sophia was in his arms, kissing him hungrily, caressing him, letting him know she wanted him. He reached down and his fingers caressed the warm, smooth skin of her inner thighs. When his fingers traveled up and found her moistness, intense excitement ran through Mitch causing his body to spasm. His mouth returned to hers, the kiss grew deeper and deeper as Mitch took all of Sophia's sweet, juicy tongue into his mouth. He rolled Sophia onto her back and it was his turn to straddle her, never breaking the kiss. Shudders ripped through Sophia's body as his lips moved from her mouth to her breasts again where he nibbled, bit and sucked impatiently on her delicate, creamy flesh. Sophia felt breathless, lightheaded. As her young, firm yet soft body shivered, Mitch held her as though he would never let her go.

It wasn't until Mitch attempted to enter Sophia's slick wet vessel that he realized she hadn't been loved by a man in that way before. He hesitated a moment, waiting patiently, carefully searching her face for a sign that this was what she really wanted. He had to be sure. He felt he owed her that much. When Mitch saw the desire burning in Sophia's eyes, a desire absolutely matching the smoldering coal of his own needs, he couldn't help but wonder did

Sophia really want her first time to be a one night stand with someone she had just met, someone who was married and would probably never see again, someone who could only offer her one night of passion. Sophia answered his unspoken question with a kiss filled with all the passion she possessed. A kiss that unmistakably said yes. Not only did she want him, she knew she needed him. Sophia removed her tongue from his mouth long enough to whisper into his mouth, "Please, Mitch. Please let me have you."

Her pleading caused Mitch to moan out loud as they fell deep into another kiss, devouring each other. Tears swam into Sophia's eyes just knowing she would get what she hoped for, what she wished for, even prayed for.

Mitch entered her sweet wet cavity again with Sophia responding as if she had been waiting for that moment her entire life. His body seemed to know her body already and his firm taut lines fit her soft smooth curves perfectly. Once Mitch was inside Sophia and began plunging deeper and deeper into her, he watched her face transform into something of wonder. Sophia was receiving something very special for the first time—something that she had wanted for a long time, but just wasn't really sure what to do with it. It was like the greatest mystery of her life, unfolding before her eyes. She moaned out loud from a combination of unfamiliar pain yet undeniable pleasure. This was something she had never experienced before—a whole new adventure and she wanted to be a part of it all.

Mitch moved in and out of Sophia, her body becoming more encouraging and as she received him, he began to quicken his pace. Soon, she found a rhythm that began to match his and she gave herself fully to him. Sophia gripped Mitch's ass cheeks and held on tightly as her young, energetic body met his now powerful thrusts.

Throbbing with desire, Mitch thrust himself deeper and deeper into Sophia as her body moved frantically around on the sheet. She clawed and gripped him like the jaws of a vice, wanting more and more of him. Mitch's powerful, lean body obeyed the command to have Sophia completely and in kind, she responded like some magnetic needle quivering, moving towards the heart of his masculinity.

Their bodies were in perfect sync as they moved together. The sounds of their flesh smacking together propelled them into greater heights, in outer space, arousing them beyond their imagination. Their passion for each other became insatiable. As much as they took of each other, the more they felt they had to have. Mitch and Sophia were being guided by a force greater than their own. Sophia began to soar and as she did, she screamed his name. Mitch! Mitch! Mitch! Over and over again. Mitch plunged into the depth of Sophia, taking her with all the frustration and pent up anger that he had carried around inside him for much too long. He drove his male hardness into her, relentlessly, unyieldingly with each of them becoming lost in the unbelievably passionate and incredibly satisfying intensity that neither had experienced before. They were lost in their kissing, overwhelmed by their touching, and they were weakened by the onslaught of passion they were unleashing on each other. The feeling was so incredibly powerful, the way Mitch reduced Sophia to a total loss of control caused her head to swim. Then, after seizing everything the other gave, together in a shattering, blinding, consuming heat, the secret core deep inside Sophia exploded and showered her body with sparks of sensation with her responding like a beautiful butterfly bursting out of a cocoon.

Mitch and Sophia fell apart to catch their breath. While Sophia flirted, it was all in good fun for Mitch but as they talked, they bonded which developed into a sexual chemistry for each other willing them to give into their own animalistic desires. By all standards, Sophia was hard to ignore; sporting a beautiful tan and a sexy beach body.

"Are you okay?" Mitch asked, trying to steady his breathing. "I hope I didn't hurt you."

As Mitch's body rested against Sophia's, she kept her eyes closed, enjoying the feel of his well-built body pressed against hers and she wanted to hold onto that feeling forever.

For years she could only imagine what it would be like to love a man that way. There was nothing she had read or heard about had prepared her for what she had just experienced. There was no way that she could've ever imagined anything so beautiful, so earth shattering, so magical, but there it was. Tonight, she had actually shared that experience with Mitch, an older man who was married and she couldn't have been more excited. He was her first and she wouldn't have had it any other way. As Sophia looked down at Mitch's magnificent body covering hers, she wondered had she pleased him, would he want to make love to her again.

Their breathing became a little less erratic now and their pulses began to return to normal. The room became still, quiet. There was no longer any movement, no panting or moans and groans. Mitch slowly opened his eyes. He had to assure himself that he had not been dreaming. With Sophia lying naked against him, he knew he had not been dreaming.

Suddenly, Sophia giggled and said, triumphantly, between gasps, "See. I was right, wasn't I?"

Still breathing heavily, Mitch lifted his head and gave her a puzzled look before rolling over onto his side to face her. "Right about what?" He asked. "What are you talking about?"

A small smile curved her lips as she lazily ran her hand across his chest. "Remember our conversation the night we saw that falling star?"

"Yeah," Mitch said, wiping sweat off his forehead with the back of his hand. "You made some kind of wish, didn't you?" Mitch closed his eyes. "Wishing on a falling star and expecting that wish to come true is silly. It's just plain crazy. I don't believe things like that. " With his eyes tightly shut, he moved his head from side to side on the pillow, trying to gather his thoughts. He began to think about what had just happened.

"Yes, and my wish just came true."

Sophia's words pulled Mitch from his moment of reverie. Not only did he give Sophia a surprised look, but there was a lift of surprise in his voice when he asked, "So this is what you wished for?"

"Yes. When I saw you earlier tonight, I knew that I wanted you to be my first."

"Why?' His breathing less erratic now.

"You stood out from everyone else in the place."

"Now, that surprises me."

"It shouldn't. You just don't know what you have to offer. You are just such a man and already I'm crazy about you."

"And, you're such a little tease," Mitch said without looking at her.

"Call it what you want but that was my wish and I am so happy that my wish came true," she said, looking down at his splendid body with its rippling muscles under smooth brown, sweat drenched skin. Then, she changed the subject, "It felt so good being in your arms, Mitch." And, she added in a whisper, "it felt so damn good."

Mitch didn't respond.

"You did want to make love to me." She was smiling but she meant it.

Mitch looked down at her and her smile was so alluring that he responded by pulling her to him again. She giggled softly. She sounded completely happy as he pulled her silken body over his hardened one. She moaned from the sheer pleasure of his touch, the way his body felt under her own. He kissed her again. His mouth was brutal on hers, hard and downright greedy as he swallowed her gasps. His lips moved from hers to toy with the tender spot of her throat. Then, his mouth snaked its way down to her breasts that were waiting for him to bite and lick and suck. Before long, they were drawn into a special place again, a place that held only the two of them in that moment.

When Mitch was inside her again, he throbbed with desire. Sophia's body held him snugly and as their movements increased, each was caught up again in a whirlwind that was dizzying. As he cupped her shapely hips, lifting her to him, he had to wonder how was it that this young woman aroused something in him that was different—something that was foreign. The wildness about Sophia, the fire in her eyes when he was making love to her, the exciting, passionate edge that she brought to their lovemaking drove Mitch out of his mind and he couldn't seem to get enough of her

Making love to Sophia the second time, their bodies dancing on the sheet, moving rhythmically together, Mitch didn't know how it felt for her but for him, he thought he felt the earth move. Their bodies were still hungry and thirsty for each other in a way that was indescribable as they sought and reached fulfillment so intense it was overwhelming. Mitch's own desire for

Sophia was overwhelming. He wanted her and he would take everything she had to offer. He didn't know what he would do when it was time to say goodbye to her. The thought of leaving her, caused him to plunge into her with shocking velocity. Mitch thrust harder and harder like a ferocious animal, going deeper and deeper into Sophia until his body shuddered with one final, very forceful thrust. Sophia's eyes rolled back in her head as her body exploded in mind-bending, earth shattering climax before they collapsed in each other's arms.

After a moment, Sophia positioned herself so she could see Mitch's face.

"I love you," she said breathlessly.

Mitch had to admit. Sophia was like a beautiful, wild animal roaming free and who gave far more than she took. She aroused something in him that he hadn't felt in an entire lifetime, but what he was feeling for this young creature certainly wasn't love, was it? No, of course not, he answered his own thought. Mitch wasn't sure why he and Sophia connected on some basic level that really didn't make much sense to him. He could deny it all he wanted to but these was some strong underlying chemistry between them and strangely it had been there from the moment they met. Or could it be that Sophia was there, she was willing and eager and almost insistent on having him and he simply took what she wanted him to have.

Mitch sat up and threw his legs out over the side of the bed. Sophia caught his shoulder and tried to pull him back down in bed beside her.

"I've got to go," he said.

Disappointment flashed across her face, but it was gone quickly and she gave Mitch a smile that seemed to say, it was okay. Mitch got up from the side of the bed and he quickly dressed.

"Are you sure you can't stay a little longer?" Sophia asked quietly, giving him a provocative look as she hugged her pillow.

It was now Mitch's turn to give her a look. He glanced over his shoulder and said,

"No, you know I can't." He reached across the bed for her hand.

She threw the pillow aside, and pulling the sheet around her, she accepted his hand and he helped her as she crawled out of bed and stood in front of him. "I really enjoyed being with you tonight," she said, softly, smiling up at him.

His face was void of emotion when he replied, "So did I."

"Tonight was so special for me."

Mitch knew exactly what Sophia meant. He was the first man to touch her in that way. "I know," he acknowledged. "For what it's worth, tonight was special for me also."

As if she hadn't heard him speak, Sophia began to explain to Mitch what being with him tonight meant to her, "I know your situation, that you have another complete life away from here, you belong to someone else, but I wrapped my heart up in a bow and I gave it to you for you to do with whatever you want. My heart belongs to

you now, so please take good care of it."
Sophia moved up close to Mitch, she kissed
him just above his heart, then laid her cheek
against the spot.

Mitch didn't know how to respond, so he
said, "Walk me to the door, please?"

Sophia slowly walked with him toward
the door, allowing the sheet to fall from her
body to the floor. Mitch felt his heart thump
against his ribs as he looked at Sophia's
body that was nothing short of perfection.
She felt him grow hard against her and she
slid her arms around his waist, holding him
to her. He reached out once more and
stroked a rosy nipple ever so gently and felt
it spring into instant life. Sophia's hand slid
down and touched Mitch between his legs.

He gave her a look as he moved her hand
away and collected himself. "You are such
a bad girl," he said, looking down at her.

Sophia giggled as she stood with him at
the door. He was anxious to get out of there
before he found himself back in Sophia's
bed and enjoying all that she was so willing

to give him all over again. After Mitch kissed Sophia one last time, he eased out of the room and closed the door behind him.

It didn't take Mitch long to walk back to his hotel. When he entered his suite, he wasn't surprised that his wife was nowhere in sight. And, from the looks of things, she hadn't returned since she left. Mitch quickly removed his clothes and shoes. After brushing his teeth, he stepped into the spray of the shower and allowed the cool water to wash away the sweat, the guilt, the sin, and the shame that seemed to cling to his body. Closing his eyes, he leaned into the water and as his mind recaptured the events of the night, he wondering how he could have allowed something like that to happen. Sophie was gorgeous, sexy and naughty and he had been intrigued by it. If his own wife were a quarter of the woman Sophie was toward him, what took place between he and Sophia tonight would never have happened. He knew that with every fiber of his being. There was something to be said about a person not being satisfied at home.

Sophia's zest for life and her fiery spirit energized him in a way that he couldn't explain—in a way that he had not experienced before, and the strange thing was that he found himself attracted to it— perhaps a little too much. She was the kind of girl who could become addictive, Mitch thought.

Mitch twisted off the shower and toweled himself off. He walked nude back into the bedroom, collapsed in the sheets and within minutes, he was asleep.

* * *

Kaline emptied her glass and placed it on the table she shared with her companions. They all seemed just as tired as she was, but none of them would admit it. The group included Jason and his second wife, Anita, their cousin Mark, his girlfriend Michelle and her sister Naomi. Observing them Kaline shook her head shamefully. Yes, they had definitely had a great time all night, but she had witnessed some things that made her feel terrible about how she had been treating Mitch.

She kept recalling how much Anita had literally begged Jason to buy her a drink and the fact that Mark simply ignored Michelle's requests, but drank whatever her sister brought to the table, was just unacceptable. These women were falling all over Jason and Mark when they didn't seem to care about them. Mitch, on the other hand, would have been waiting on her hand and foot.

Glancing at her watch, Kaline saw that it was after five in the morning. Last night had been something else. Sure, the dancing and the drinks had been great with her new friends, but Kaline had to admit that compared to Michelle and Anita, she was living the life of a pampered queen. She felt terrible.

Grabbing her purse she hurriedly told her companions it was time for her to go. It was due time she apologized to Mitch and treat him the way he deserved to be treated. Mitch was not the kind of man who'd sit down and take her abuse forever, and she certainly didn't want to lose her man to another woman.

Kaline hurried towards the bank of elevators in the hotel's lobby. She knew she'd find Mitch sound asleep in their suite. Guilt swept through her as she thought about the boring night that he must have had, alone and lonely in the room. She could just kick herself for how selfish and stubborn she had been.

Exiting the elevator on their floor, Kaline shook her head dejectedly; she needed to make Mitch know how much she appreciated him. She couldn't run the risk of him finding pleasure or appreciation in the arms of another woman!

CHAPTER 5

Mitch awoke to the smell of coffee and bacon.

"Mitch," he heard Kaline call out his name. "Wake up, sleepy head."

"Good morning to you too," Mitch said, unsmiling and without opening his eyes, he added, sternly, "You're not gonna start this day off unjustly taking out your frustrations on me by berating me. It's not gonna happen. You've been making my life hell and I'm not gonna do this with you anymore. If you can't accept that I'm doing my best, there's nothing else I can say. Just go on and do what you have to do." The words had tumbled out of Mitch's mouth before he closed his eyes again.

"I'm not going to give you a hard time, baby. I love you," Kaline said softly.

Mitch felt a gentle kiss on his lips and his body jerked involuntarily. Quickly, he opened his eyes and was startled to see Kaline bending over him, smiling.

"What's wrong, honey?" she asked, smiling into her husband's eyes. "You look as though you've seen a ghost."

Mitch sat up in bed, the covers falling from his chest down to his waist, remembering his anger and disappointment with his wife's behavior on last evening. Only now, he was even angrier and disappointed with himself because of what he had done last night, with Sophia. Sophia, he thought. She was back in his mind again. A total stranger. A beautiful and loving stranger, but still a stranger. Mitch ran a hand down his face. *What have I done*? He thought, staring at Kalina. Mitch had never cheated on his wife before last night. But, back in the suite, secure in the knowledge that his dirty little secret would be just that, a dirty little secret, and he would never see

Sophia again, he had to admit that Sophia touched something inside him that no one else had, not even his wife, and the sex had been incredible. For the brief moments they were together, it was as if it were just the two of them, alone in the world.

Then, realizing what he was thinking, he quickly shook his head to clear it of those thoughts. He never wanted to think of Sophia again—ever. Why would he when he was still so much in love with his wife.

In a quick movement, Kaline pulled back the drapes, flooding the room with the late morning sunlight. She slightly opened the patio door allowing the sound of the waves crashing against the shore to float into their ksuite. "I ordered breakfast for us. See," she offered. "Sausage, eggs over light, strong black coffee, toast and your favorite, grape jelly." She showed him the display of breakfast that sat on the serving table in their room near their bed. "Come, have some breakfast with me."

"You're in a good mood. Can I ask what brought this on?" Mitch wanted to know.

"That's it exactly. I am in a good mood. Now come on. Get out of bed and let's eat. Breakfast is getting cold." Mitch gave Kaline a strange look but he obeyed, tossing back the covers and getting out of bed. "What?" She gave him a little laugh. "Why are you looking at me like that?"

"I'm just wondering who are you and what have you done with my wife."

Kaline gave a little chuckle. That was the first that she had laughed with him in a while. "Honey, I'm sorry for the way I've treated you. Of course you didn't deserve it and I'm truly sorry that I wasn't there for you as I should have been, but if you will forgive me, I promise I'll make it up to you." Mitch was staring at his wife. She noticed. "Honey, I said I'm sorry. Why are you looking at me like I have three heads or something."

"I was just thinking what a complicated woman you are," he replied, going over to the table and taking a seat where Kaline had arranged the placement of their breakfast.

Kaline walked around the table to where Mitch was sitting. She bent down behind his chair, dropped her hands to his bared chest, allowing them to gently glide down to his navel. "And you love every inch of my complicated self, don't you?" she teased, reminding him of the old Kaline that he loved so much.

"There has never been any doubt about that. It's just that as long as we have known each other, I still don't know where you are coming from sometime."

"I know, but--" Kaline began, with regret lacing her voice.

"We're just gonna have to do better," Mitch interrupted hastily, "because all this arguing gets to be too much."

She silenced him with a soft kiss and then whispered against his mouth, "Shut up and eat." Kaline walked back around the table and took her seat across from her husband.

Mitch looked at his wife's smiling face for a moment. "You're looking damn good this morning, baby," he said, looking at her and appreciating what he saw.

He winked at her before he reached across the table and took one of her hands in his. He leaned across the table and pressed his lips against her fingers. "I've missed you."

"I know, baby but all that is history now. Your wife is back."

Mitch looked at Kaline for a long moment. Then, he smiled and after buttering a piece of toast, he spread grape jelly on it and before he took a bite he offered one to her.

During breakfast, Kaline talked about the people she had met, she apologized for not spending more time with him, "and," she said, "I promise to make it up to you." When he didn't respond, she turned her head to find him staring unblinking at her. "Are you still angry at me?"

"No, not anymore."

"I'm really sorry, Mitch. I know I hurt you with my words sometime, and I'm wrong to do that. But, like I said, I'm gonna do better. That's a promise."

Mitch got up from the table, walked around to his wife's chair, and he thanked her with a deep, passionate kiss, just like the ones they shared before coming to the beach. Kaline ended the kiss with a suggestive look in her eyes. "Let's skip the rest of our breakfast. I want you. I want you now," she said, getting up from the table and began peeling off her robe, exposing her shapely body. Mitch complied avidly by lifting her from the floor and carrying her over to the bed. He lay Kaline down on the bed and took her mouth in a savage kiss.

While his tongue ravaged her mouth, his hands ravaged her body. They groaned and whimpered out of pure pleasure, but nothing compared with the electric sensations Mitch's fingers evoked when they slid into the wet triangle between Kaline's thighs. After using his fingers on her and kissing her until her lips began to feel bruised, they made incredible, fervent, ground moving love.

Afterwards, Kaline said, half smiling while trying to catch her breath, "Oh my goodness! What's gotten into you? If I didn't know better, I'd think that you were thinking of someone else just then." She turned over on her back and looked dreamily at the ceiling. "I've got to make you angry more often, babe because that was incredible."

Mitch wasn't gonna touch that comment. Besides, his head felt like someone had hit him with a hammer. And, groggy from lovemaking, two thoughts occupied his mind. Why had he been such a fool last night and made love with a stranger and, second, why hadn't his wife behaved this way all along?

The next few hours passed in a blur. Mitch and Kaline stayed in bed most of the day, making love between meals.

"Why are you so good to me?" she asked, running her fingers across his forehead.

"I don't know. Maybe because of all the little things I love about you."

"Good answer," Kaline said and they chuckled.

A short time before sunset, an exhausted Kaline untangled herself from her husband, pulled herself out of bed, dragging Mitch along with her into the bathroom where they stepped into the shower together.

"Oh doggone it," she groaned, letting her head fall on her husband's chest.

Mitch had already begun lathering his body with the hotel soap that was available to them. "What's wrong?" he asked, pushing her back so he could look in her face.

"I'm out of soap. You know I've got to have my special soap." She held up a sliver of what was left of her favorite scented soap, unlike the kind that the hotel offered.

"You want me to go out now and get soap?"

"I packed only the one bar that I had left and it's just about gone. See." She lifted it up to show him again. "I meant to pick up some before we got here."

"Hotel soap won't do for just one shower? We could go out later and get you some."

"Honey, I hate their soap. You know that," she said, looking sheepishly at him.

"Alright, alright." Mitch said, dripping as he stepped out of the shower and grabbed a towel. After drying off, he slipped into a pair of pants and a pullover shirt and after checking with the hotel clerk about the location of a local bath and body shop, he left the hotel.

Mitch drove the short distance to a bath and body shop. He parked near the shop, removed his seat belt and got out of the car. Whistling happily, wanting to make the purchase and get back to his beautiful wife

155

who was waiting for him, as he was approaching the door to the Bath, Body & Beyond store, a familiar voice called out to him, interrupting his reverie.

"Hello, Mitch."

Mitch turned to see Sophia across the street, waiting for the stop light to change so that she could cross over to where he was. Mitch's eyes popped out of his head, his jaw dropped, his body became frozen.

The light changed and Mitch stared unbelieving at the young woman walking across the street towards him. The adrenaline was pumping like a speeding locomotive through his veins. He took a deep breath. The closer Sophia got to Mitch, he wondered just how old she really was… or rather, how young she was. He studied her as she approached him. When she reached Mitch, before he could alter her movements, she bounced into his arms wrapped her arms around his neck and kissed him on the mouth. "Good morning, Mitch," she cooed, smiling up in his face.

"Sophia," Mitch began, nervously, his entire body getting cold and clammy. He pulled Sophia's arms from around his neck and he backed away from her. He studied Sophia for a moment. She was flawlessly dressed in white shorts with matching halter top and beige sandals, looking like she had just stepped from the pages of a fashion magazine. In the light of day and without wearing makeup, Sophia looked to be about eighteen, nineteen at the most. Mitch couldn't believe his eyes. He also didn't want to be in an embrace with a woman less than half his own age, but more importantly, he didn't want to be seen in the company of any other woman. He was a married man, a very happily married man. "What are you doing here," he asked, glancing around to see whose eyes might be staring at them.

A huge smile on her face, Sophia said, happily, "I am so happy to see you. I was hoping we would see each other again." Then, smiling wickedly at him, she added, "Last night was hot. I enjoyed our time together so much."

Sophia quickly went into Mitch's arms and kissed him again, thrusting her tongue deeply into his mouth. Mitch hurriedly removed her arms from around his neck, moved back away from her and looked around, again.

"Yeah, last night was great," Mitch mumbled, "and it is nice seeing you again, but I'm in a hurry. You take care, alright." Mitch walked toward the door of the store to make a purchase for Kaline and he hoped Sophia would go on about her business, but no such luck. Sophia followed Mitch and caught his arm to go into the store with him. Mitch stopped just outside the door, removed her hand from his arm and looked intently at her. "Where are you going? I've told you I'm in a hurry and I don't have time for this today."

Sophia's heart froze. She denied the ache that floated in her chest. She didn't understand why Mitch was being so mean to her, so blunt, so cold, a complete opposite of how he treated her last night. Sophie felt an eerie sensation, like the breath of the devil himself. She swallowed hard against the tears she felt were getting close to the surface. Fixing him with a stare with hurt touching her beautiful eyes, she was trembling when she asked, "What's wrong, Mitch? I know you enjoyed being with me last night. I could feel it and so did you. We made as connection. You can brush it off or ignore it all you want but the reality is that feelings were there and they were real."

The bath and body shop wasn't far from the hotel Mitch and Kaline were staying and Kaline liked the beach and taking long walks and Mitch didn't want to run the risk of his wife running into him and Sophia. "What are you doing? You know we can't be here like this. I'm married, Sophia, and I am in love with my wife. You know that and you know we can't be doing this, especially not in public." He used his hands to make a sweeping gesture. "And," he looked away, "last night was a mistake, a terrible mistake. I'm sorry if you expected more but there's nothing I can do about that. Now, go on, get outta here."

Sophia's heart was pounding painfully in her chest as she held his gaze, couldn't believe this was the same man. Mitch met her gaze with an even stare. He took a deep breath. Then the more he despised himself for his behavior, the more the frown on his face deepened.

"You have to understand that I don't want to be ugly with you and whatever happened between us last night, it's wasn't important. We were just two people who apparently needed each other and we took advantage of that. That's all it was. You have to forget it and get on with your life." He gave her a dark and angry look.

"I don't want to forget you, Mitch." Sophia quickly wrapped her arms around Mitch's neck again, intending to kiss him again.

Mitch ripped Sophia's arms away and firmly held onto her hands. "You have to."

"Mitch, please don't do this."

"Grow up and stop behaving like a child." He let go of her hand and ran his hand across his forehead to remove the perspiration. Mitch was having difficulty swallowing the lump that had formed in his throat. He looked up toward the sky for a moment before returning his eyes to meet hers. "You are a beautiful young lady. You shouldn't have any problems finding a nice young man to love you the way you deserve to be loved, but," he finished his statement in a softer tone, "it can't be me. Last night was great. I enjoyed it, but it's over. I'm sorry."

"Why?" She reached for him again and again he held her hands, restraining her.

"Sophia, what are you? Twelve?" Mitch asked rhetorically but Sophia responded.

"No."

"Have you been listening to anything I've said?" he said, sarcastically, squeezing her small hands tightly. "What are you not getting?" He cleared his throat and took a deep, calming breath. "Look, I don't want to hurt you. I really don't. I think you're a nice girl, a really sweet girl, but I have a wife who I love very much, she loves me and there is no room in my life for anyone else. I'm sorry, but I'm done with this conversation. "You got that?" He released her hands so violently that time that Sophia almost fell.

Gathering her composure, she said in a childlike voice, "I thought you loved me."

"Love you?" Anger flared in Mitch, he threw his hands in the air and again attempted to open the door to the store.

Sophia followed him with quick, short steps. "That's what you told me last night. Don't you remember?"

Losing patience with her, Mitch said, "What the fuck are you talking about? How could I love you when I don't even know your little ass? You knew what you were getting yourself into, going after me the way you did. It was you who came on to me and in an aggressive manner, I might add, so don't start acting like I owe you something because I don't owe you a damn thing. Now, get loss."

Shocked by his tone, but Sophia steeled herself against the deep emotion in his voice. She unconsciously twisted her slender hands together, while thoughts ran furiously through Mitch's head, how he should never have left his suite last night after he first arrived there. How he definitely never should have gone back over to Sophia's room. He wished he could go back in time and hit the reset button, make different choices. He also wished he could kick himself in the ass for being so damn stupid. Mitch stared at Sophia and asked, "How old are you anyway?"

"Old enough," Sophia replied brightly. She was quick to tease him and though her heart was breaking into a million little pieces, she managed to smile.

Mitch gave her a stern look. "We are not going to play these games anymore. Tell me how old you are, Sophia!" he demanded. "And, this time, don't give me some off the wall bull shit. Tell me the truth, damn it."

"I am sixteen, but," she pouted, "I'll be seventeen in a month."

"What the fu--?" Mitch roared, but stopped himself from completing his question, his eyes piercing her. He didn't believe what Sophia had told him, didn't want to believing it. Blood was rushing to his head. "You're sixteen?!" he asked incredulously.

"I am sixteen," she repeated, a little smirk touching the corners of her lips.

"Sophia, this is not a joke so don't you play with me." He lifted a brow. "Are you honestly telling me you are sixteen years old?"

"Yes."

"You've got to be kidding me." Shaking his head and looking up at the sky, not only could Mitch not believe what he was hearing, he couldn't believe how stupid he had been. "You are just a kid!" Mitch was pissed off with Sophia for initiating the situation that took place between them but at the same time, pure unadulterated shame washed over him. He knew she was young,

164

but sixteen. "What have I gotten myself into," he mumbled under his breath. There was nothing about Sophia that would lead Mitch to think that she was that young. He squeezed his eyes shut and he shook his head again. "I'll be damned," he whispered.

He had been wrong about Sophia. He had been stupid on so many levels. His face tightened. He groaned and cursed silently. The darkened atmosphere of the club, the makeup, the drinks he had consumed and the invigorating feeling he got when he was around Sophia were very potent ingredients that had contributed to him guessing she could have been in her mid twenties.

Mitch turned another cold stare on Sophia. "Do you know what the authorities would do to me if they knew we slept together?" he asked and he angrily hurled the answer to his question. "They would put my black ass underneath the jail house."

"I'm not going to tell anyone, Mitch." He heard her words, but why didn't he feel any better. "I don't want to get you into trouble," she said in a small voice.

"Well, thank you for that. You take care," he said and was about to walk away.

Then Sophia changed the subject. "Can we have a cup of coffee somewhere?"

He looked at her. His face tightened even more as he snarled, "Are you out of your mind? Look, my wife is waiting for me and I've gotta run. Have a nice life."

"Who are you?" Sophia gave Mitch a disapproving look. She thought he was a nice man, a caring man. Could she have been that wrong about him? "I don't know how I could have thought you were so special, so different. How could I have been so fooled by you? You told me last night that you and your wife were having problems. You said you didn't think that she loved you anymore."

And, I need my dumb ass kicked, Mitch thought, struggling to compose his features as he replied, "Well, I was wrong. Look, young lady, Sophia or whoever the hell you are, I don't have any more time for this." He used his hand again to wipe away more perspiration that gathered on his forehead and turned to walk away.

"Would you mind if I shot you an e-mail or text sometime?" Sophia asked innocently, reaching for his arm.

Mitch had developed patience dealing with clients and even more so dealing with his wife, but now his hard-earned patience was sorely waning. He turned and fixed his narrowed eyes on her face. What the hell is this, he thought. Had he gotten himself into some real life fatal attraction? "Are you kidding me right now? You are treating this situation like some kind of joke and it's not. I'm done with it. You and I will never see each other or talk to each other ever again. You got that?" Mitch raised his hands in exasperation, "I'm outta here." He turned and walked away from the bath and body shop and Sophia, but not before he saw tears gathering in her lovely, sad eyes.

Sophia's locked her hands together and tears slid down her face. She watched as Mitch walked blindly across the street where he had parked the rented Volvo, climbed into the car and rested his head against the seat with his gaze fixed on the young girl he had cheated on his wife with, the girl he had just treated like shit. She was just a child and she had looked small, lost, devastated, standing alone on the sidewalk, so unlike the sophisticated Sophia he'd met last night. Mitch's heart went out to her.

Mitch knew in his heart that he had played a huge part in her pain and most of all, he knew that he owed her. If no more than an apology, he owed her. Sophia was so unpredictable and already believed she was in love with Mitch. There was no way of knowing how she would have reacted to seeing Mitch with his wife or any other woman. Mitch knew that he had to put some distance between himself and Sophia. He couldn't risk running into her again, especially if Kaline was with him.

Mitch blew out a frustrated stream of air before he twist on the ignition and drove away, gunning the engine. Blinded by tears and cradling her head in her hands, Sophia was left alone with only the memory of her one night stand with Mitch and the faint scent of the cologne he was wearing.

Sometime later, Mitch entered his hotel suite where his wife was waiting for him. After his unpleasant encounter with Sophia, he needed to give himself some time to think. He had to drive around a while to clear his head before returning to the hotel and Kaline. Mitch's encounter with Sophia that morning cleared up some of the things that had crossed his mind. There were times last night when they were spending time together, Sophia appeared naïve while other times, she was more sophisticated than people who were much older than she. Never would he have imagined her to be sixteen. Mitch began to perspire all over again. Additionally, he had to locate another bath shop to get his wife's favorite soap. It was out of the question to return without it. The last thing he needed was to get into another argument with Kaline. If he thought that bout with Sophia was difficult and stressful, a confrontation with Kaline would be like World War III and today, he couldn't handle it.

"You got my soap?" Kaline greeted Mitch at the door, took the bag from his hand and looked inside the bag to see several bars of her favorite soap. She smiled brightly. "What took you so long?" She stopped when she saw the look on his face. "What's wrong?" she asked.

"Nothing. I am fine," he replied, but his thoughts were disjointed and jumbled. If only he could think straight. If only he could concentrate beyond what he had gotten himself into less than twenty-four hours ago.

"You look as if you've seen a ghost." Kaline laughed.

Mitch's jaw clenched but he gave a weak laugh. "I am just fine," he lied.

"Okay." She accepted his answer. "Well, I am going to take my shower. You can join me if you want."

"Go on. I'll be there in a minute."

"Are you sure you're okay because you don't look so good. I hope you're not coming down with anything."

Mitch was sweating. He used both to wipe the perspiration away. "I'm good," he said.

Kaline gave her husband a perplexed look before making her way to the shower.

Why did he have to run into Sophia? She was the last person he had expected to see or wanted to see. Mitch walked over, flung open the door and stepped out on the terrace. Holding his breath, he looked up and down the beach, hoping not to see Sophia. Seeing no sign of her, he exhaled, went back inside and joined his wife in the shower. Two days later and having no further run-ins with Sophia, Mitch and Kaline happily packed their bags and headed home.

A year had brought on significant changes in Mitch and Kaline's lives. She made good on her promise to Mitch, especially when six months later, he became partner in the firm and was making a salary comparable to his position. With his new income, their first big ticket item was a new home. It was their turn to live in a nice neighborhood, in a fabulous, pricey home. They had gone from living in a 3000 square foot house to a small mansion located in the same gated community where her friend, Tracy, lived. The home offered an Oprah Winfrey type closet, two master bedrooms with adjoining bathrooms, Jacuzzis, custom tiles in the showers and his and her sinks. With Kalina's insistence, they'd even bought a two bedroom cabin on the lake. They had money in the bank. They were moving up the financial ladder of success.

Their social life had improved tremendously; they had joined a couple of country clubs, went to the best parties, dined at the most elegant restaurants and they vacationed at fabulous locales. Mitch and Kaline had gone through financial struggles and she had never failed to remind him of what an epic failure he was. They had arrived and he finally had been able to please his wife, providing her with her hearts desires. It looked as though their dark verbally abusive days were behind them.

CHAPTER 6

On Memorial Day, Mitch and Kaline had spared no expense on a huge backyard barbeque for their friends. Their doorbell had been ringing nonstop that afternoon as a stream of invited guests moved through the house to the backyard where the festivities were happening. Kaline answered the front door and after taking more of their guests outside, she returned to the kitchen for another platter of food.

"So, that's what you're up to. I don't know why you didn't have the whole thing catered. It would have been a lot less work for you, honey," Mitch chuckled, watching her remove a platter of meat from the refrigerator to be placed on the grill.

"Almost everything was catered but for a backyard barbeque, you men like to fuss around with the grill," she grinned. "I'll be finished with this in a minute, if that doorbell would quit ringing." She gave that wonderful, throaty laugh that Mitch loved so much. "Maybe we should put a sign on the front door, saying, "Please come to the back of the house," she used her fingers to signify quote, unquote. Mitch joined in with his wife's laughter. She handed him the tray of meat. "Take this outside for me, please."

Mitch left and returned within minutes to find Kaline unwrapping cakes that had been sliced and laid out on a tray. She picked up a piece between two fingers. "Come, taste a piece."

Mitch approached her and she popped a small piece of cake into his mouth, then her own. "Ummm!" Mitch said, swallowing his cake. Then, taking Kaline into his arms, he kissed most of her cake out of her mouth. He broke the kiss. "I'm going to grab some more beer and haul it outside," he said as the front doorbell rang again. "Oops, there it goes again," Mitch said as he and his wife lifted their hands in the air.

Kaline chuckled. "Please get that for me."

"Yeah, sure." Mitch headed toward the front door.

"Mitchell Jamel Harding," Kaline called out to her husband. He turned and looked at her. "I love you," she said, sweetly.

Mitch smiled, shook his head and headed toward the door. Kaline resumed what she was doing so that she could rejoin the others outside. Mitch ushered other guests out to the backyard. That was not the last time the doorbell rang. It did so several more times within minutes of each other. After escorting another group of guests to their backyard, Mitch said, "Baby, I think I'm going to take your advice and put up that sign on the front door."

"That's what I would do." Kaline chuckled, licking her fingers and pulling more condiments from the cabinet above the stove while Mitch rummaged through a drawer for paper and a marker to make the sign for the front door.

"There. That should do it," Mitch said, satisfied that his artwork would solve the nonstop ringing of the front doorbell. After fishing a roll of scotch tape from a drawer, he went with his sign through the foyer to attach it to the door.

Mitch had been gone a while before Kaline called out to him, craning her neck, looking towards the front door, "Honey, come give me a hand with this dessert tray." Not getting a response, she placed the knife on the counter, and wiping her hands on a dish cloth, she made her way to the front door. "Honey," she said, pulling the door wide open. "What's taking so long to put up a simple sign? Oh," she said, and flashing a broad smiled, extended her hand to their latest guest who was carrying a baby in a bassinet. "Hi, I am Kaline Harding. Welcome to our home."

She shifted her eyes from the young woman to the infant. Kaline's eyebrows shot up, her smile froze. Her first thought was, who is this young woman on her doorstep with a baby who looked remarkably like her own family? Could Evan have fathered this child and now this young woman came in search of him?

Barely able to tear her eyes away from the baby, Kaline asked, "Can we help you?" Then, looking at Sophia again, she inquired before the young lady could respond, "Do you know Evan, our son?" Kaline cast her eyes at the baby again, then the young lady. But, what puzzled her was when she looked over at Mitch and he looked as though he were having a stroke.

"No, I have no idea who your son is," the young woman began, looking Directly into Kaline's eyes. "My name is Sophia Hartford and I here to see Mitch Harding." Then, looking at a dumbfounded Mitch before thrusting the bassinet she was holding into his hands. "This is our son. His name is Mithell Jamel Harding, Jr."

Kaline's hands flew to her mouth. Her body sagged with numbness, completely devoid of energy. She gave Sophia a dark look before her questioning gaze came to rest on Mitch, who looked as though he would pass out any moment.

Mitch looked at his wife, her eyes pierced his. Initially he saw confusion. As knowledge registered in Kaline's eyes, he saw disappointment, pain. She couldn't possibly know the details of what happened between her husband and Sophia, but Mitch was certain Kaline knew the baby was the result of his indiscretion with someone other than her. Mitch felt a stab of agony, like a dagger piercing through his heart. He couldn't think, speak or breathe. He could only look on helplessly, knowing his life as he knew it would never be the same. He also knew his day would get increasingly worse.

"I carried our child for 9 months and cared for him until today. It's your turn now."

With that Sophia turned and walked away as Mitch and Kaline watched her climb into the back seat of a sleek late model black sedan. As Sophia's car drove away, she didn't give Mitch and Kaline a backward glance but she did leave them with the truth. The trouble with truth is that it can change everything.

When Sophia's car was completely out of sight, Kaline closed her mouth that had been gaping open and collected herself enough to turn a hateful eye on her husband. Then, shaking her head in disbelief, she asked, "What the hell was that, Mitch? What have you done?" Her eyes danced from her husband's to those of the child who lay in the bassinet. "Answer me, damn it. What the fuck have you done?" Completely oblivious to the guest who continued to arrive for the backyard event, she didn't care that they heard her nor did she care what they thought of what she was saying. "I'm waiting."

Totally dumbfounded, still holding the basinet, Mitch stuttered, "I..I don't know."

"What do you mean you don't know?" Not waiting for Mitch to respond, Kaline pointed both hands in the direction of the baby who was playing peacefully in the bassinet. "Damn it, you'd better have some answers because you've got a lot explaining to do. Now, I want you to get rid of all those damn people," she pointed towards the back yard, "because I want to hear from you how something like this could've happened." In a huff, Kaline turned to go back into the house. Then, as if the life had suddenly drained out of her body, she turned back to Mitch. "How could you do this to me? How could you, Mitch?"

Mitch looked helpless as Kaline turned, and inside the door, she gave him one more hateful glare before slamming the door behind her. Not only was he completely shocked about what had just happened but what was that strange sensation that settled in the pit of his stomach at the sight of Sophia. Mitch took the baby inside the house and sat the bassinet atop the kitchen counter. He went outside through the kitchen door. Kaline didn't know nor did she care what apologies he made to dismiss their guests just as long as he did and get back inside to face her music. Mitch re-entered the kitchen to see Kaline sitting at their kitchen table, weeping wildly. She looked up as he stood with his back against the door. She leaped from her chair with such force that the chair was knocked to the floor as she rushed up to her husband and began pounding him in his chest with both fists. "You son of a bitch. What have you done?"

Mitch caught both of her hands, restraining her blows. "Calm down, Kaline."

"Calm down my ass," she screamed, unable to loosen her husband's grip on her wrists. "How did you get involved with that child and have a baby with her? And don't you even try to tell me that child isn't yours." She glanced over at the baby in the bassinet. "Because that child looks exactly like you. He looks more like you than our son."

Mitch hated to admit it but he knew what Kaline said was true. One look at that baby and anyone would know who his daddy was.

"Who was that girl?"

"No one."

"Who is she? How long have you known her? Does she live around here?" The questions flew out of Kaline's mouth. "And, the way you looked at her just then. Don't think I didn't catch that. What's up with that, Mitch? Who was that girl, that child?"

"I never meant to hurt you, I swear."

"Didn't you think that sleeping with someone would hurt me?"
"I'm so sorry."

"That much is absolutely correct," she sneered as she tried to free her hands again. "You are sorry. Now, let go of me!"

"I will let you go if you calm down and give me a chance to explain."

After struggling some more and unable to free herself of his grip, Kaline calmed down as much as she was able to and she sat back down. After a moment, Mitch released her hands. He removed a glass from the cabinet, pulled a bottle of Scotch from another cabinet and poured himself a drink. He gulped down the liquid before he pulled out a chair and sat at the table across from his wife.

"You remember when we went to Myrtle Beach last year and you didn't have time for me? You partied with a bunch of strangers, leaving me alone in our suite."

"What are you talking about?" Kaline screamed at Mitch.

"I wanted to do was spend time with you." Mitch closed his eyes and threw his head back. "I'm only interested in you, Kaline. I love you, but I got caught up and I need you to forgive me. I have to make you forgive me."

"Good luck with that."

Mitch ignored that comment. "Are you gonna let me tell you what happened or are you gonna scream at me all day?"

Kaline settled back in her seat and glared at Mitch.

Mitch had a tightening in his chest, but he cleared his throat and began talking and he didn't stop until the whole sordid story was out.

"What do you want me to do with that?" Kaline snapped. "What should I do with what you've just told me?"

"I don't know. I know I don't have the right to ask anything of you, Kaline, but all I can say is I am sorry and I hope we will try to work through this? I made a horrible mistake. I need to have my ass kicked. I know that, and I'll take anything you want to do to me but please, please don't give up on me, on what we have. I don't want to lose you."

"I would leave your ass for the infidelity alone but you have thrown not only an underage girl into the mix, you brought a baby into our marriage on top of everything." Kaline closed her eyes and shook her head as if to rid the ugly thought running amuck in her mind. "You must think I am some kind of a damn fool."

"No, baby. I don't think that at all." Mitch got up from his chair and walked over to where his wife was sitting. He reached for her hands but she drew her arms tightly across her chest. He kneeled on the floor beside her chair. "Kaline, please."

Tears were still falling down Kaline's cheeks.

"Don't cry, please. Baby, I am so sorry. Please forgive me."

"You took me on vacation and you didn't want to do a damn thing but stay coop up in that hotel room and because I went out to have a little fun, you took your old ass out, get all turned up with some little underage bitch, you get her pregnant and now that baby is here in my damn house?" Kaline hissed. She was so angry that her body was shaking in her chair.

"Kaline, I was wrong, and I'm willing to take responsibility for what I did but I am asking you to let me make it up to you, please? I love you so much. You know that. Things just got crazy and I failed you. We now have everything we worked so hard for. Our life is good. Our life is great and if we could build on that......
Kaline, if we care about each other as much as I believe we do, then we should at least try to save that."

Kaline looked at Mitch as though he had three heads. "Are you serious? Do you think there is something left between us that can be saved? If you really think that, it only shows what a messed up perverted ass you really are."

That remark stunned Mitch. "Do you really think so little of me? I'm human,

Kaline. It happened one night. I've never cheated on you before or since. It was a mistake. I don't know how many times or how many ways I can say it. There's no excuse for what I did. All I can say is that it just happened."

"Do you have any idea what this girl's parents could do to you for what you did to their daughter? If she even has parents. What kind of decent parents would have a daughter get involved with a married man who is more than twice her age and gets herself into this kind of trouble?"

Mitch didn't respond. He allowed Kaline to vent.

"You fucked a kid, Mitch." She squinted up her face as though it repulsed her to speak the words. "Who does that? No one, other than some old ass perverted man who wants to feel good about himself."

Mitch had heard enough about how perverted he was. "Damn it, Kaline, none of this would have happened if you had treated me with a little respect. It was really what you did, how you behaved, that caused me to do what I did. I work hard, I provide for my family and all I wanted to do was get away for a bit, relax and spend some quality time with my wife, but you weren't having any of that." Mitch lifted his shoulders in a helpless gesture.

"You are blaming me for what happened?"

"No, I'm not. I'm just trying to explain how this happened.. I went to a club, I had a couple of drinks and," he paused. "Well, you know the rest."

"How would you feel if I'd gone out and fucked some random stranger while we were on vacation?"

Mitch looked his wife squarely in the eyes. "I really don't know that you didn't, Kaline. You indicated as much."

"Fuck you." Kaline shot Mitch a hateful look, getting out of her seat. "We're done here."

"Just take it easy," he put his hands on her shoulders, forcing her back in her seat. "Let me fix this. Please."

"I'm gonna make this real simple for you. There's no way for you to fix this. There's no way for you to undo all the misery you've created," she yelled, her eyes dancing with more anger than he had ever seen from her. She raised up from the chair again, this time not allowing Mitch to restrain her. "Look, I am done and now I want you to get your ass out of here and take your little bastard with you." Kaline was about to leave the room.

"Come on, Kaline. Let's not do this."

"Just get out, Mitch."

Mitch sighed heavily, then he relented and threw up his hands. "I'll sleep on the couch tonight and we'll leave in the morning."

"I want you out of here tonight, both of you. And just so you know, getting rid of me is not going to be a picnic because I

189

intend to get paid. I will screw you over six ways from Sunday. Keep that in mind, Mr. Sexy," she hurled sarcastically as she stormed out of the kitchen.

Even when people made stupid choices, Mitch believed they had the ability to turn them around and do the right thing. It was obvious Kaline didn't share that belief. Mitch packed a bag and he and the baby left the house. He put the baby in the back seat of his car and after strapping in the car seat, Mitch drove to a nearby hotel and checked in.

That was almost six years ago. Mitch and Sophia's one night stand had lead to a life that combined lust and betrayal into an explosive concoction. That one night of weakness was enough to do great damage and it had. Mitch seldom saw Kaline after that day, she filed for a divorce and as soon as the divorce was final a year later, she got married again. This time, she married a politician, her friend, Tracy's brother.

Mitch went through the process of buying a house, setting up a nursery in the home for the baby, buying clothes, obtaining a pediatrician for his son, and he secured a competent nanny. While the nanny cared for Mitch's son, he left his old firm and started his own business. It seemed everything he touched turned to gold. His real estate listings were extensive. It wasn't long before Mitch had so many projects in the works that it was necessary to double his staff to reduce his load. And though he was the owner of his company, he had volunteered to head up many of the out of town training sessions for his new brokers.

***

"Dad."

"What is it, son?" Mitch answered his six year old as he drove him to the day care.

"Why don't I have a mommy?"

Although Mitch knew he and his son would have this conversation one day, still he was a little taken aback when it happened. That was the first time the subject of Mitch Junior's mother came up since Sophia dropped off their son a little over six years ago and left. They hadn't heard a word from her since.

"Why do you ask, son? Aren't you happy with our lives' our home, living with just me?"

"Yeah, Dad, I do but all my friends have a mommy. Their moms take them to ball games, to movies and the park, and they play video games," Mitch Junior explained, "they have pizza and eat hot dogs."

Mitch looked over at his son. Over the past years, he had concentrated so completely on starting his own company and making a success of it that he had not devoted as much time to his son as he now realize he should have. Mitch had been devastated after Sophia brought his son into their lives, Kaline threw him and the baby out of the house and later divorced him. The only woman who had been in Mitch Junior's life on a consistent basis was Mrs. Lucy, their live-in nanny and housekeeper.

Mitch loved his son from the day he met him but it was Mrs. Lucy who practically raised Mitch Junior. She had taken him to his medical appointments, school programs, and Mitch Junior owned so many toys and backyard playground equipment that he spent an enormous amount of time entertaining himself at home.

"Well, son," Mitch began, "every child does not have a mother and a father in the home. Some kids have a mom and no dad while some others have a dad and no mom, but what those parents try to do is give their child so much love so that the child doesn't feel that anything is missing. I know you would like to have a mommy, but God didn't work it out that way for us."

"Like Missy and Kevin," Mitch Junior replied. "They only have a daddy but they don't have a mommy."

Mitch wasn't sure how else to handle the situation that his son just presented him with. He said," I was thinking about going over to the park on Saturday and throw a few balls to my favorite son. What do you think about that?"

Mitch Junior's face broke out into a huge grin. "Really? You and me?"

"You and I," Mitch corrected, grinning and added. "Yeah. You and I will get up and after we have breakfast, we will go wherever you want to go; a park, movie. Whatever."

"Can we have breakfast at IHOP?"

"Sure we can, Sport."

"Yeah, I love that restaurant. It's one of my favorite places to have breakfast."

Mitch didn't know that was his son's favorite breakfast place. "Sure we can have breakfast there. That's one of my favorite restaurants also."

"Cool."

As Mitch drove through the busy early morning traffic, he reached over and ran his hand over his son's head as they grinned at each other.

After a moment, Mitch Junior said, "I bet you didn't know that Miss Scarborough likes you?"

"What? No, she doesn't," Mitch, with a frown on his face, glanced over at Mitch Junior. "Miss Scarborough?"

"Yes, she does."

Miss Scarborough was a young, attractive teacher at the day care that Mitch Junior attended. "Why do you think Miss Scarborough likes me?"

"Because she does."

"I don't think so," Mitch drove expertly through the early morning traffic.

"Yes she does."

"How do you know that?"

"Because when you dropped me off yesterday, I heard her talking to Mrs. Barbey about you."

"She did. Were you eavesdropping on them? You know it's not polite to listen in on adults' conversation or any conversation that doesn't involve you, right?"

"I know that and I wasn't. I was just walking by them, going into my school."

Mitch was quiet for a moment. Then, he asked, "Well, what did Miss Scarborough say to Mrs. Barbey....about me?"

"She said you were hot." What did she mean by that, daddy?"

Mitch smiled. "I'm not sure. What do you think she meant by that?"

"I think she likes you."

"You do, huh?"

"Yeah. She said something else too," Mitch Junior said shyly.

"She did?"

Mitch Junior glanced at his father, then he looked down at his hands. "She said she wouldn't mind getting with you. Doesn't that mean she likes you?"

"She was probably just making conversation. I don't think she meant anything by what she said."

"Okay," Mitch Junior said and turned to look out the window.

Mitch chuckled quietly to himself.

When Sophia brought Mitch Junior from New York to Philadelphia to Mitch, he believed Sophia was promiscuous even after he found himself to be the first one to breach her barrier. There was no way that he was the only one who had her. And after the way that they parted he figured that she would have drowned her sorrows in boys her own age. Yet even thinking this way Mitch never had a DNA test done on Mitch Junior. Not only did the child have Mitch's eyes, he knew this was his child. That he had absolutely no doubt about.

Mitch pulled into a parking space in the school's parking lot and switched off the engine. He removed his seat belt, got out of the car and walked around to the other side. With his book bag in hand, Mitch Junior jumped out the car and he walked with his father towards the door to the school, waving to teachers they past with Mitch noticing the look he got Miss Scarborough.

Mitch arrived at work a few minutes before nine and he was able to accomplish an enormous amount of work before heading home. He loved the look in his son's eyes when he entered their home shortly after five that afternoon.

"Dad," Mitch Junior exclaimed, leaping out of his seat at the table where Mrs. Lucy was assisting him with his homework, and he rushed up to his father, "You're home. Do you have to go back to work?"

"No. I'm home for the rest of the day. What are you and Mrs. Lucy doing?" Mitch asked.

"My homework."

"You want me to help you finish that?" Mitch offered and winked at his housekeeper as he acknowledged her. "Hello, Mrs. Lucy."

"Yeah, Daddy."

"Good afternoon, Mr. Harding," Mrs. Lucy smiled and returned the wink as she got up from the table and headed to the kitchen to finish making dinner.

"When we get through, we can go bicycle riding for a while," Mitch said, putting his brief case on the table. He removed his jacket, hung it on the back of a chairs and he sat down next to his son. "What do you say about that?"

"But you don't have a bicycle," Mitch Junior wrinkled up his face as he looked at his father.

"Yes I do. I bought myself a bike today."

"Is that true?" his son squealed. "What color is it?"

"Fire engine red."

"Like mine?"

"Just like yours."

"Oh man."

Mitch rolled up his shirt sleeve and his son finished his homework. Afterwards, they changed into casual clothes and after donning their helmets, they hopped on their bikes and rode off together.

"What do you say we stop off and get an ice cream cone before coming back home?" Mitch asked his son.

"I say yes," Mitch Junior grinned.

"If Mrs. Lucy finds out we had ice cream before dinner, we're gonna be in deep trouble," Mitch said laughing. Mitch Junior snickered as they continued to ride along together on their bikes.

Mitch and his son returned home after more than an hour riding their bikes around the neighborhood and eating ice cream cones. They parked their bikes in the garage and entered the kitchen with Mitch saying to his son, "Go get washed up for dinner." Mitch Junior dashed off toward the bathroom. He stopped and turned when his father called out to him. "If we get through with dinner in time, we may be able to watch a movie."

"Yesss," Mitch Junior said, running off to the bathroom.

* * *

"Miss Hartford, you have come a long way and you are making remarkable progress. It takes time for someone to recover from the challenges you have experienced but it is wonderful to see that you are making great strides in your recovery, both physically and emotionally," Phia's therapist said to her.

"Dr. Mattison, I can't tell you how much I appreciate your help through all these years, first as my therapist and as my friend and confidant. Thank you so much."

"I can see how well you are doing emotionally but how are you feeling now physical?"

"For the first time in my life, I am feeling like a real person, almost whole."

Dr. Mattison nodded her head back and forth in understanding.

"I still have a few things I need to work out in my life and I believe then I believe I will be the person that I want to be...complete."

"You said the most important thing to you is that you want to be in your child's life, that you are going to make that happen."

"I have been without my child too long and believe it or not, I need him. He doesn't need me but I need him and more importantly, I want him."

"And you still have not been in touch with your child's father?"

"No."

"Do you have some sort of plan of how you intend to reintroduce yourself into your son's life through his father?"

"No, I haven't put any thought of how I am going to do it. I just know that I will, and it won't be long."

"Are you still in love with him? The father, I mean?"

"Yes I am."

Dr. Mattison looked at Phia and smiled. "I believe you are now ready to take that step to reconnect with your son and the part of your past life that you want. I am

confident you will make it happen. Good
luck with whatever you decide to do with
your life."

"Thank you Doctor."

Dr. Mattison pushed back in her high
back swivel chair behind her huge
mahogany desk and laced her fingers
together before saying, "You are going to be
just fine, Phia. Just fine." Then she placed
her hands on her desk and said, "If you need
to come back in the next month or so for
whatever you feel you need, please don't
hesitate to set up some time with my
assistant."

"I will and thanks again for everything."

"You are welcome. Now, go live your
life. Enjoy!"

"I will," Phia said and after a warm
embrace between the two women, Phia left
her doctor's office with a huge smile on her
face.

CHAPTER 7

The cab stopped in front of Angelina's, a posh New York City night club and restaurant. Phia stepped out of the cab wearing a long sleeve white blouse and tight black straight leg pants that hugged her amazing curves like a glove and black sling back shoes, and she walked into the entry way of the restaurant. It had been years since she met with her friends to hang out and have some fun. Three months ago Phia's days consisted of doctor's appointments, taking medication, chemo treatments and weak and sick to the point where she found herself heaving while bent over a toilet. For years, her body had been downright exhausted. But now that she had had her final chemotherapy treatment, she was eating regular meals and had regained some stamina. Phia was feeling on top of the world, and tomorrow she was going out of town to give a speech at a cancer awareness seminar. But, tonight, she was meeting Afrika, one of her best friends, and they were going to turn up.

Phia and Afrika had been best friends since elementary school and although they had not seen each other in nearly four years, they had kept in touch. Throughout the years, Phia and Afrika had shared all their secrets. Well, all their secrets, except one. Phia had never told Afrika the circumstances surrounding what had happened to her child.

When Phia entered the semi crowded restaurant and she and Afrika saw each other, the two young women raced to each other and embraced.

"Africa," Phia said, happily, as she and Afrika released one another. "How are you?"

Just as happy, Africa replied, "I'm fine, Phia. It's so good to see you. How long has it been?" she asked as she reached up and touch Phia's hair that she now wore much shorter.

"Girl, too long," Phia replied as she removed a tissue from her purse and touch it to her eyes.

"Don't cry," Afrika said, squeezing Phia's hand.

Once they were seated, Afrika reached across the table, touched Phia's arm and asked, "So how are you doing?"

"So much better now, girl. My last round of chemo is over, I'm not tired and feeling all yucky anymore," Phia said. "That thing just wore me out, but I'm just grateful that it's over. I've got a clean bill of health."

"And, you're now cancer free."

"Yep. Cancer free," Phia said and smiled.

"I'm so grateful that you are and you look fantastic."

A waitress approached, took their lunch orders and returned shortly with iced tea for each of them.

"You've been through so much," Africa said before taking a sip from her tea glass. "Having the baby alone, the cancer, chemo, and you've come through all of it so well. I am so happy for you and so damn proud of you."

Phia smiled. "Thank you." Then she said, "Girl, I'm so happy to see you. I've missed you so much."

"I know and I've missed you." After a moment, Afrika said, "I wish I could have been there for you. You know that, don't you?"

"Of course I do but how could you? We were both kids when all of this began. We were seventeen and that was when you and your parents moved away?"

"When daddy's job took him to Oregon, I thought my life was over," Afrika said and they chuckled. "Really, I thought I would never see you again. But, Phia, tell me, why did it take you so long to tell me what was going on with you?" Afrika wanted to know, concern clearly displayed on her pretty chocolate colored face.

"I didn't want to worry you. I knew there wasn't anything you could have done at that time and as time passed, all I could think about was trying to work my way through the hand that I was dealt. But, all is well now. I feel terrific and all is well."

"Hopefully, we'll never be far apart again," Afrika said, then added, "When you get back from your seminar, we are going to go out and turn all the way up."

"That sounds like a plan. I'm ready for that. I haven't done anything in quite a while." Phia looked at her friend.

After a moment, Africa placed her hands, with her fingers laced, on the table and asked, "How is your boy?"

"As you know, I'm not in his life but I still keep up on him from a distance. There are some things that I didn't tell you about my son. My son's father was married but he's not anymore. His wife divorced him and he's never remarried," Phia said and when she was finished, she had told her friend all of the circumstances surrounding her son.

"You hired someone to keep tabs on what was going on with your son?"

"Yes, with momma's help and with all the negatives things that have happened, there were equally as many positives. As luck would have it, there was this wonderful housekeeper and nanny who used to live in my neighborhood and took excellent care of my neighbor's children. Later, she moved to Pennsylvania, Philadelphia, in fact. The city where my baby's father lives to be closer to her daughter. As it turned out, she is now my son's live-in-housekeeper," Phia smiled widely. "When the investigator reported to me who my son's live-in-nanny was, I ecstatic because I knew my child was in excellent hands. I know what sort of man my son's father is and that he would do absolutely the right thing by our child no matter what he felt about me. So, as I said, I know my baby is just fine."

"That was more than luck. I'd say someone upstairs is looking out for you. Girl, you're something else." Africa smiled and gave Phia a high five across the table. "That is quite a story?"

"My son is in daycare now but will be entering the first grade this fall. His daddy is making sure that things are fine with him."

"You took a huge risk in what you did. Did you ever think your son's father would give him up for adoption?"

Without a moment's hesitation, Phia replied, "No. Not for a second. In spite of everything he and I went through, I think my son's dad is a really good person who was trapped in a bad situation, a very uneven marriage. He was soured about his marriage which is partially what brought us together anyway. He treated me badly but I believe he's been treated badly as well."

"With everything that happened, I believe you've loved that man all these years."

"I've thought of him every day since we met."

Africa chuckled.

"What's so funny?"

"I was thinking that you went gangsta on his ass when you put him on blast back then."

"Don't laugh, girl. I should have handled the situation better, but once I wrapped my head around my new reality, knowing I couldn't take care of my baby or myself, I couldn't think of any other way of handling it. That's not an excuse, just a fact and with momma's help and Mitch just being the man that he is, I knew my son would be alright."

Africa reached across the table to touch her best friend's hand again. When she released Phia's hand and reclined back in her seat, she asked, "Do you think you'll see your son and his father again?"

"You bet your ass I will," Phia said without hesitation. "My son's father hates me like crazy but I'm going to be a part of my son's life. I don't know how I'm going to do this, but some way, somehow, I'm going to make it happen," she finished, her voice trailed off as she looked out across the restaurant.

"And knowing you, Phia, it will happen," Afrika said, pulling Phia from her reverie. "You are one of those women who once you get something in that mind of yours, look out."

They chuckled.

"Well enough about me. Tell me what's going on with you? How are things with you and Jeff?"

"Jeff. Now, that's another story, Phia. Being involved with a married man was never anything I aspired to do. Never wanted to be the other woman, you know."

"When you told me Jeff was married, I was surprised because you were never about that life."

"I guess I am now."

"I don't know why when you learned Jeff was married, you didn't just put him in your rear view and kept it moving."

"Is this the pot calling the kettle black," Afrika chuckled. "It was the circumstances under which Jeff and I met. By the time I learned he was married, I was already in love with the damn man. That shit just slipped up on me. I'm just keeping it one hundred. That's how I roll."

Phia shook her head as both of them chuckled. "I know, and you know I'm not judgmental. Especially, with what I've done, and even though you've always done things out of the box, I never figured you to be the other woman, the woman who was willing to share a man. You going after a married man was surprising to me. For one thing, I know you're not a fan of sharing your man. This is something different for you. Where do things stand with you and Jeff now? I know you two love each other. I know it was not an ideal situation, but at least your situation is one that you can see, be a part of in some small way, have sort of a relationship with even though perhaps you can't say it's completely yours. Who would've ever thought that you and I, precious little socialites that we were, would ever get involved with married men instead of the kind of men our parents would want us to be involved with?"

"Jeff loves me. I know that but being the married man that he is, he doesn't have much time for me and that leaves me lonely and sad."

"You two are still just seeing each other once a week?"

"Pretty much except on rare occasions, he will come by during the week for an hour, maybe two. You know Phia, I have asked Jeff on more than one occasion to let's just go off somewhere and spend twenty-four hours together, but he can't seem to find that much time for me."

"Africa, that's not asking too much. You have the right to want and demand to spend a little time with your man. Why is he not giving you what you're asking for?"

Their meals were delivered; Cornish hen, baked potato and green beans for Phia and Prime Rib, baked potato and corn, with a basket of rolls.

"If Jeff is not at that job that he loves more than the food that he eats, he is doing someone a favor. You know, helping family or a friend or putting in even more hours at his job. I don't know whether being the CEO of his own business is a blessing or a curse. I tell you, Phia, if I weren't so in love with that man, I'd be long gone because a lot of guys are at me and they certainly could beat his time."

"But you are not interested in any of those guys."

"No, I'm not and there's the sex. The sex is awesome. He really knows how to lay it down."

"I see. You're in love with what's hanging between his legs?" Phia laughed.

"You got that right."

"Are you two planning anything before the summer ends?"

"Well, he's in Vegas with his wife now. They vacationed several times a year and I get one night maybe once every other month."

"You know how I feel about that. I told you before that that's not fair. He's got to be more considerate of you than that. If you're gonna continue to spend time with him, you deserve so much more than that. And, I know, he takes on the cost of your condo, he buys you jewelry, nice clothes, shoes and he gives you all kinds of money, all of which you already have, but if he can't give you some quality time, then I don't know." Phia lifted her hands in the air in a helpless gesture.

"That is one of the reasons I'm still with him other than the fact that I'm so much in love with him."

"Well, when he gets back in town, you need to have a sit down for a heart to heart with him. You've just not demanded anything from Jeff, Africa. You are that easy going, care-free type. Sometimes you've just got to lay your cards on the table. Girl, tell the man what you want. Don't allow him to make all the decisions; when he's going to see you and what you two are going to do. You don't have to follow his rules. You two are in this relationship together and you two should make the decisions together. Don't give away all your power and you know you got some power, girl." Phia winked at her friend and they giggled some more.

"I know. It's a crazy kind of love, the kind that that doesn't completely do you right yet it doesn't leave you alone either. As I said, it's crazy, but I just don't like to put any pressure on Jeff. He gets enough of that at home. That woman has it made and I don't even think she knows it or appreciates the great lifestyle she has for that matter."

"I am not in the least concerned about what's going on in Jeff wife's life. You are my friend, my best friend and I want you to be happy. You told me some time ago that you don't want to get married yet and that all you wanted to do was date Jeff and have him take care of you financially. Have you changed your mind about that?"

"No, and I know you think I'm crazy but for now, I don't want a husband. Jeff does a lot for me. He has helped me to start my beauty treatment spa and it is doing really well. It's a full service spa where women come in and have a nice glass of wine while getting full beauty treatments."

"Ouch," Phia said and they giggled.

When Tracy stopped laughing, she said, "right. You know, the works. Come in tired, rundown and grumpy but leave recharged, restored and reinvigorated."

"One stop beauty shopping, huh?" Phia said and they both laughed.

"You got it," Africa said and laughed some more.

"Putting some things aside, you've got a pretty good situation going for yourself. You don't have to stay on the grind all day, you make a boat load of money, your man does take wonderful care of you, he sends you on great vacations," Phia said, but Africa interrupted.

"Yeah, vacations that I take alone or with friends."

"I know, I know," Phia said but she was thinking she would give up everything she had if she had the love of the man she fell in love with the day she met him and that had not changed.

"What's up, bitches," Phia and Afrika's heads snapped when they heard that familiar voice near their table say.

When they saw their friend, Diamond, both ladies leaped from the table and the three women embraced. "Diamond, where did you come from? Are you back in New York now?" Phia asked as she released her friend.

"We wanted to surprise you," Afrika said.

"You two surprise me alright. You two are gonna make me lose all of my makeup," Phia teased and brushed away tears that had formed in her eyes and began to flow down her cheeks. "What have you been doing?" She asked Diamond?"

"This and that," Diamond answered, giggling and added, "Look at you two, looking all fly and fabulous."

"How long have you been in town?" Phia wanted to know, unable to disguise her excitement at seeing her two best friends. "Here, sit and have something to drink." She pointed to a chair at the table.

Diamond sat and the girls began to catch up with her getting the details on Afrika's married boyfriend and Phia's cancer survivor situation.

"We still haven't heard what you've been doing the past few years," Phia said.

"One of those old Frenchmen got her nose open," Afrika said.

"What? If any nose gonna be open, I'm gonna be the one who does the opening. Girl bye," Diamond replied, laughing. Diamond rose out of her chair. "We'll catch up on everything later but right now, let get out of here and get our party on. I want to dance with some good looking boys, have a couple of good drinks and turn up," Diamond said.

As they were leaving their table, two couples entered the restaurant.

"That's some good looking man meat right there," Diamond said and they laughed.

"Obviously the girls with them think so too." Phia laughed.

"There's nothing more attractive than another woman's man," Diamond commented.

"They are just kids. You're almost old enough to be their mother," Afrika pitched in.

"Yeah, they do look kinda young," Phia said.

"When has that ever stopped me," Diamond said.

"She's got a point," Afrika said.

"Come on. We've got so much to catch up on," Phia said.

"Yeah, like what have you been doing in France all this time?" Afrika questioned Diamond.

"Nosy heffas," Diamond giggled. "Seeing you bitches again is like old times."

Giggling, the three ladies left the restaurant with their arms around each other.

* * *

"You remember that I will be out of town a couple of days at a meeting, right?" Mitch reminded his young son.

"I remember," his son said. "You're going to Chicago."

"That's right."

"What are you going to bring me from your trip this time?"

"That's going to be a surprise."

"Ahhh, dad."

"You know the rules, Sport. When I go away, I always bring you a mystery gift. We don't talk about the gift before you receive

224

it, right? But I'm willing to bet you're gonna like it."

"Alright," his son said and forked the last bit of scrambled eggs into his mouth.

Just then, Mitch's housekeeper, who was also the babysitter for Mitch's son, entered the kitchen, carrying two bags of groceries that she set down on the counter.

"I see you two are still here," she said. "Mitch, Jr. are you ready to see the animals?"

"Yes, and I'm really excited too," he replied.

"Yes, he got up practically at the crack of dawn, Mrs. Lucy," Mitch said to her and they chuckled, then to his son, "come on, Sport, drink your juice so we can go. You don't want to be late for your field trip, do you?" Mitch said, looking at his young son whose eyes were an exact replica of his own. The boy's hair was sandy, he was intelligent beyond his five years and he was already teaching his father computer games and was winning more often than not.

"No, dad. My teacher said we're going to have a lot of fun." His son took a huge swallow of his orange juice.

"Is that what Mrs. Barbara said?"

"Yes. She said we're going to see all kinds of animals. The giraffe is my favorite animal." His son turned and looked at his father. "Why is the lion your favorite animal, dad?"

Mitch thumped his chest with both fists. "Because the lion is the king of the jungle."

"But the giraffe is bigger."

"You've got a point there, Sport." Mitch gave his son a high five.

"So you'll be back from your meeting in Chicago day after tomorrow?"

"That's right, son. And you be a good boy and mind Mrs. Lucy alright?"

"I will dad, but you did say I could stay up on Friday night. Did you tell Mrs. Lucy that I could stay up late?"

"Yes, I did." Mitch smiled at his housekeeper who returned the smile. 'But only until 10:30, and don't forget to brush your teeth. Now come on. Grab your backpack and let's get this show on the road."

"Bye, bye you two," Mrs. Lucy said. "Have a nice trip, Mr. Hardin."

"Thanks, Mrs. Lucy."

Mitch's son hurriedly put on his backpack and headed for the door. After passing his father in the foyer, the young boy shouted, "The last one out the door is a nasty stinking rotten egg."

"That's no fair," Mitch said, hurrying after his son. "Cheater!"

When they arrived at Special Times Day Care Center, Mitch shut off the engine, got out of the car and ran around to the back passenger door of the car.

As he opened the door to the car, his son was trying to unbuckle the belt to his car seat. "I can do it dad."

Mitch smiled as he watched his son fumbled with his car seatbelt. Seeing the difficulty his son was experiencing, he said, "Let me give you a hand there, Sport." Mitch unhooked the seatbelt, lifted his son from the seat and placed him on the concrete sidewalk. After closing the door, they walked up to the entry door to the center.

Mitch's son rushed ahead of his father and reached for the door knob. "Daddy, I can open the door."

Because the door was heavy, Mitch knew his son wouldn't be able to open it without help. "Okay, but let me help you with that. I'll bet in a short while, you'll be able to open any door you want."

"Okay," he replied happily.

They entered the building to see Mrs. Barbara standing in the hall with two other teachers. When she saw Mitch, Jr. and his father, she said to the teachers, "Alright, we should be ready to leave in a half hour." Then she turned to Mitch and his son and said, as she approached them, "Good morning to you both."

"Good morning, Mrs. Barbara," Mitch Jr. said, jubilantly.

"How are you this morning, Mrs. Barbara?" Mitch greeted, pleasantly.

"There's Bobby, dad." Mitch Jr. was about to rush off to his friend.

"Hey, wait a minute. Aren't you forgetting something?"

"Dad." Mitch Jr. turned to his father and gave him a high five before rushing off to join his friend.

"No running," Mitch called after his son. Then he said to Mrs. Barbara, "So you'll be back here around 2 o'clock?"

"Yes." Mrs. Barbara glanced at her watch. "We'll leave for the zoo in about twenty minutes, and we'll spend a couple of hours there, then take them to McDonald's, feed them and bring them on back here. So he'll be ready to be picked up at the usual time," Mrs. Jackson said.

"Sounds great," Mitch replied. "Well, see you later." With that, he left the building, got into his car and drove across town towards his office. On the drive, an old song played on his car radio. It was a song that he and Sophia danced to the night they met. *Sophia.* Mitch had to admit that he'd thought of her often, well, almost every time he looked at his son. His mind would wonder to that night years ago when he'd held her in his arms, the way she'd wrapped her body around his and held him as though he was the only man on the planet.

Mitch and Sophia were together more than six years ago, when she was sixteen. He'd tried to not allowed himself to think of Sophia in a sexual way. But now, although he was forty-something and she was no more than twenty-two, he had to wonder what her life was like now. Did she drop out of school to have the baby? Did she go back to school afterwards? Was she married? Was she happy? Did she ever think about the baby—or him? Mitch had a lot of questions, but he only had one answer. Sophia was a very pretty girl when they met but a year and a baby later when Mitch had last seen her, Sophia was absolutely gorgeous.

Mitch pulled his navy late model Lexus into his parking space outside his office building and took the elevator up to the fifth floor. In his office, he checked in with his secretary, made a few phone calls, then he left his office and drove to the airport.

When Mitch was on the plane, he located his seat and opened his briefcase. He removed a folder before closing the case and sliding it under his aisle seat. He removed a pen from his jacket pocket, opened the folder and began reviewing his notes. It wasn't long before a flight attendant announced that all seats were to be put in the upright position and prepare for landing.

Mitch, along with more than a hundred other passengers exited the plane. He made his way through the crowded airport to the outside where he checked his watch, and noted he had less than an hour before his meeting. He hailed a taxi and went to the hotel where his meeting was being held and where he would be staying the next two days.

Mitch arrived at the hotel, took the elevator up to the twelfth floor conference room with only minutes to spare. After a short meet and greet with the new realtors, they all gathered around the huge conference where agendas were placed on the table and the meeting began.

About more than an hour had passed, Mitch got up from the table and left the conference room. He took the elevator down to the fifth floor where he knew there was a cigarette machine. He was walking down the hall toward the concierge's room when suddenly a conference room door opened. Mitch was startled. Not by the two women rushing from the conference room and whisking by him. It was the voice of the speaker coming from that room—a voice that sounded awfully familiar. That couldn't be who he thought it was, yet he had to see. He had to be sure.

Mitch opened the conference room door to a room filled to capacity. He eased into the room and he turned and looked in the direction from where the familiar voice was coming. There she was in all her splendor. Sophia! Mitch was frozen in his tracks. He felt the anger that he'd harbored for years flared with an even greater intensity. He must have had shock written all over his face because when the two women who left the room earlier returned, one of them gave him a very odd stare while the other asked, "Sir, are you all right?"

"Ye, ye, yes," he stuttered. "I'm fine." He turned slowly, left the room and he took the elevator back up to the twelfth floor but not before he'd made a note of the time Sophia's conference would end. Five o'clock.

When Mitch re-entered his conference room, the rest of the afternoon went by in a blur. He was grateful he'd done his presentation before he went out in the hall and saw Sophia because now, he could not focus on anything that was happening in his conference room. His only thought was of Sophia's beautiful face, her makeup flawless with lips that perfectly matched the soft pink suit she was wearing. The copper hair that once hung below her slender shoulders was now not much longer than the pixie cut Mia Farrow wore years ago. Hair or no hair, Sophia was even more gorgeous than she was six years ago when he met her.

Day one of Mitch's meeting ended at three forty-five. They went down to the hotel dining room and ordered a late lunch. When Mitch took the elevator back to the fifth floor, he couldn't remember whether he ate the plate of prime rib, red potatoes, green beans and the salad that were placed on the table before him or did he just toy with it a moment before excusing himself to rush off to be face to face with Sophia. He'd waited for the day that he would lay eyes on her again and now she would have some explaining to do.

As he thought about her, he wondered how she would respond to him. Would she be distant, hostile, friendly? She probably wouldn't be friendly towards him, Mitch concluded. He could scratch that off his list. Why was he wondering what Sophia's behavior would be with him anyway. Why would he care? She was the one who brought the rage of hell into his home, causing his wife of more than twenty years to leave him, or rather kick him out of their home, destroying their marriage, his life. She should be the one wondering how he would treat her. Mitch had to admit that he stayed angry with Sophia a long time but the years have calmed that anger and pain somewhat. He was just grateful now for the son she'd given him.

Mitch got off the elevator and rushed to the conference room where he hoped Sophia would still be. He poked his head in the door to see Sophia shaking hands with another speaker who'd just finished her speech and walked off the platform. There was a vacant seat on the wall by the door and without taking his eyes off of Sophia, he walked over to it and sat. He looked down at his hands that were clenched together between his legs that were spread apart. When he looked up, he made eye contact with Sophia. She hadn't seen him dressed in any other attire other than the normal casual beachwear, but today, he looked unbelievable handsome and professional in the dark business suit that he was wearing. And, the years that they hadn't seen each other hadn't hurt his good looks at all. In fact, he was even more handsome than Sophia remembered, but she could see that he was very angry.

The impulse to run to him, to feel his strong arms come round her again, was so strong, so powerful that she involuntarily took a step in his direction and was stopped by another young girl who approached her and not only shook her hand but embraced her as well. Mitch couldn't deny that the look Sophia gave him made him wonder whether she'd been expecting him. Yet, how could she know he'd be there? Had she seen him when he was there earlier? She couldn't know him that well, could she, Mitch thought.

He waited until the event was over and while Sophia talked with women who went up to shake her hand. After saying goodbye to others she then put some documents into her attaché case. As people left the conference, Sophia approached Mitch assessing him all the while. He was a little older, he looked a little tired but he was still well built and still very attractive, distinguished and a little visible gray in his hair added to his sophistication. He noticed the pink ribbon on her jacket as he got up from his seat.

"Hello, Mitch. How are you?" she asked.

"I'm good, Sophia. How are you? You look great."

"I am great, Mitch and you do as well."

"I see that you were the guest speaker."

"Yes. They invited me and I was more than happy to come."

"Do you live here in Chicago?"

"No, I still live in Manhattan."

"You are a long way from home."

"You could say that."

"You do these speeches often?"

"Just the past two years. I do three or four a year."

"I was here earlier today when you were giving your speech. I caught the end of it. You were imparting some really positive messages to those women. That was wonderful to see."

Sophia looked into Mitch's eyes. She smiled at him and his heart almost stopped beating. "Thank you." After a moment, she said, "I always hoped I'd see you again. Just wasn't sure what I'd say to you." Then she said it. "How is our son?"

Mitch was completely taken aback. "Our son?" he exploded, angrily. Then his reply became a statement. "Our son. Can you really call him our son? You dropped the baby off, gave your little two second speech and you were gone. You never even call back to check on the baby, to see whether he was alright. Who does that? Hell, it's not like you didn't know how to reach me."

Sophia's eyes became very angry but she didn't respond. She knew when she left the baby with Mitch and his wife that she only brought his birth certificate, his medical records, a few diapers and outfits. She didn't bring any formula. How was Mitch to know what the baby was supposed to eat?

"How could you do that?" he lashed out. "How could you treat the baby that way?"

"I could ask how you could've treated me the way you did. You treated me like crap, I understood and I didn't hold it against you," Sophia spat out, but suddenly her eyes became very sad.

Mitch saw the sadness in Sophia's eyes
and he didn't care. He looked away. He
didn't answer that question. He knew he
treated Sophia badly at Myrtle Beach. He
didn't have to be so cruel to her so he didn't
have an answer for her. Instead he would let
Miss Sophia know that they didn't need her,
that they'd done just fine without her all
these years. He said, "To answer your
earlier question, Mitch, Jr. is fine. He's
great. He's a bright little boy. He's in
kindergarten right now but will be entering
the first grade this fall. Merlin Academy."
When Mitch looked at Sophia again, he saw
a smile touching her beautiful bee stung lips.
"You're smiling," he said.

"Mitch, Jr. You allowed him to keep
your name."

"Of course, I did. Why wouldn't I?"
Sophia noticed that Mitch's voice had
softened. There wasn't as much animosity.
"Mitch, Jr. is my son. He should have my
name." He shrugged and looked away.
There was a moment's silence, and when he
turned back to her his face had changed.
"He looks a lot like you. Some of his

mannerisms even reminded me of you. Now, his hair and his eyes, those are mine, all mine." He smiled.

"Those eyes. Your eyes. I fell in love with those eyes the moment I met them."

"The moment you met them, huh?" he said. He looked around and saw that everyone had left the room except him and Sophia. "Can we get out of here and go someplace where we can talk?"

Sophia nodded her head affirmatively. "Sure. Where would you like to go?"

"There's a little bar/restaurant downstairs. They have really good food."

"Okay. You haven't eaten?"

"I don't remember whether I ate or not. I went with others from the group, but..." he stopped short of completing his statement. When Sophia giggled again, Mitch's mind went back to the night when they met and how she giggled most of the evening at things that were funny and some of which were not so much.

They walked down the plush brown carpeted corridor to the elevator and took it to the Lobby. As they walked to the end of the hallway that opened into a restaurant with a small bar area, they entered and took a seat at the bar since all the tables in the restaurant were occupied. Mitch said, "You didn't appear surprised to see me back there."

"I was surprised when you poked your head into the room earlier."

"You saw me?"

"Yes, I did and I couldn't believe my eyes. I was so happy that I was almost at the end of my speech. I really got nervous seeing you after all these years."

Sophia got up from her seat and began to remove her jacket. Mitch assisted her with it and hung it across the back of her stool. She looked breathtaking in the sleeveless white blouse tucked neatly tucked inside the pink linen skirt. His eyes moved slowly over her long lean and curvy body before she took her seat again. When she crossed her legs, he knew his eyes lingered on the perfectly shaped legs much too long, so long that he was embarrassed when his eyes returned to her face.

The bartender approached them, dressed in sleek black slacks, a crisp white shirt and a black string bow tie, to take their drink orders.

"What would you like?" he asked Sophia.

"May I?" she asked.

Mitch lifted his shoulders and replied, "Sure."

Sophia directed her attention back to the bartender. "He'll have a White Russian and I'll have a virgin Cosmo." She turned back to Mitch. "Am I right?" She looked challengingly at him.

Mitch's lips curled at the corners in a smile. He was drinking White Russian the night he and Sophia met and she'd bought him a drink that night. "You remembered."

The bartender bowed and left to get their drinks. Sophia smiled. Her smile was so white and bright and so damn alluring that one could become mesmerized by those luscious lips. He quickly looked away. He wouldn't be taken in by that smile again. Never! He had other things on his mind, questions he wanted answer to.

"Yes. I remember everything about you, Mitch."

Mitch was surprised by that statement and all he could do was stare at Sophia, and the trance wasn't broken until the bartender returned with their drinks.

Just as the bartender brought their drinks over and was about to place them on the bar in front of them, Mitch saw a couple leaving a nearby table in the restaurant. "Hey, can you please bring those drinks over to that table?" he said, lifting Sophia's jacket from the back of the stool.

"Absolutely, Sir," the bartender replied and follow them to the table and placed the drinks there for them. "A waitress should be with you in a moment."

"Thank you," Sophia replied. Mitch nodded his approval.

When they were seated at the table, Mitch looked at Sophia. "So," he loosened his tie, "how long are you here?"

"I did my first speech today, and I have one more tomorrow. After that, I will be flying back to New York. What about you? When do you go back to Pennsylvania? You do still live in Pennsylvania, don't you?"

Mitch stared unblinkingly at her. "Yep. Same state, same city, different home." The bartender placed their drinks in front of them. Mitch picked up his drink, lifted it to Sophia and took a sip from his glass before saying, "but why do I think you already know that?"

"She couldn't handle it, huh?"

"That would be a lot for anyone to handle, don't you think?"

"I would have." Sophia looked Mitch squarely in the eyes. "I wouldn't have liked it, but I would've found a way to work through it.

Mitch looked at the beautiful young woman sitting on the stool next to his. Why was it that he believed her? Why indeed. It was simple because he knew she was telling the truth.

"You didn't say how long you will be here."

"I leave day after tomorrow."

"I see."

A waitress came to their table. She placed menus on the table. "You okay with your drinks?" she asked.

Mitch looked at Sophia who nodded affirmatively. "Yes, we're fine," he replied.

"I know you have a lot of unanswered questions, Mitch."

"You damn right I do."

"Well, before you start in on me, please let me explain. This may be hard for you to believe but I am in love with you. I've been in love with you from the moment I laid eyes on you and I've never stopped. I fell in love with your heart." Sophia paused a moment. "The cliché, love at first sight really is true. Well, let me start from the beginning. I was sixteen and my parents allowed me to go to Myrtle Beach with the daughters of my father's partner at his company. One daughter was twenty-two and the sister was my age. You know how young girls like to play dress up, wearing the older girls' clothes and makeup. People already told me I was mature for my age and I suppose I was but I was never attractive to boys my age. They were silly and immature. Anyway, dressing up, with makeup and all, it was never hard for me to go to a night club or a bar and be allowed to enter. I always fit in, looked the part. When I was at Myrtle Beach, I never got any questions about my age or got thrown out of a club or any adult venue. So it was easy enough to deceive people. I'm not saying that's a good thing but I was young and when you are young, some of your decisions are not the best." She looked at Mitch for what seemed like a long time before she said, "when I saw you in that club, whatever it was that first night, I knew right then that I wanted to spend the rest of my life with you. I felt it was destiny at least until you told me where to go the following morning."

"I know I was harsh with you and I'm sorry," he said. "That was not my normal behavior, but you could have gotten me thrown under the jail house."

Sophia continued as if Mitch had not spoken. "Several weeks after I returned home I became ill. My mom took me to the doctor and to my surprise or shock; I learned that I was pregnant with your child. Let me paint this picture for you, Mitch. I was a sixteen year old girl who is an only child to high society parents who wouldn't be caught dead having their snooty rich friends know about me and embarrass them. When they learned that I was in," she used her fingers to make quotation marks, 'trouble,' they threw me out of the house or rather, my father did. My mother put me into one of those upscale private homes for unwed mothers where I did chores and took care of myself and the baby by making sure I saw the doctor regularly, I ate properly, took my vitamins and all. Then in my fifth month of pregnancy, I was told I had cancer of the uterus and it was pretty aggressive, it was spreading through my body." Sophia heard Mitch's gasp. That gasp was much more pronounced than when she told him her parents had thrown her out the house when they learned of her pregnancy.

Suddenly, Mitch began to feel some of his anger he'd felt for years towards Sophia peel away. "You have cancer?" he said incredulously, a stunned expression on his handsome face.

Again Sophia spoke as if Mitch hadn't spoken. "Against my doctors' advice, I put off the treatments until after the baby was born. My oncologist told me where I was physically and that I needed aggressive treatments but because I wanted to give my baby the best possible chance to be healthy, I delayed treatments. I didn't want to do anything that would harm him. My mother kept tabs on me from afar the entire time. She saw to it that I had the best doctors and everything, but my dad, well, he wanted nothing to do with me."

Sophia paused a moment. "After the baby was born, they started my treatments. They gave me rounds of radiation. My hair fell out, I couldn't eat and lost a lot of weight. Radiation has some severe side effects, but not as severe as chemo. I have some great friends and their support has meant so much to me. So much." Sophia looked away thinking of the many late night, early morning calls she placed to Afrika. "When I thought I was getting better, my white cell count became elevated. Needless to say, my hope took a plunge into despair. So, I was required to have surgery and even with that, the cancer was still present. That was when they started the chemotherapy.

"The first treatments were the easiest because even though I had had the baby, my

250

body was at its strongest. But, after a few treatments, I was tired all the time. I was feverish, had a burning sensation, I was just worn out all the time. Then, one day after getting test results showing that I was cancer free, I can't tell you what that did for me."

She paused a moment. Then she said, "during all that I went through, I never stop thinking about my baby, our baby....or you. I wasn't in a position to care for him because of the treatments and the illness but I thought of Mitch, Jr. every single day and I know that one day I will unite with him. I love him very much, Mitch, but at the time, I just did what I had to do."

For the first time Mitch saw Sophia differently. Although he still had reservations about her, he also realized that he had a new found respect for the young woman. She'd been through a lot and she did so much on her own but she'd grown into an intelligent, responsible young woman and he couldn't help being impressed by her. When he spoke again, he asked as gently as he was feeling, "Why didn't you tell me that, Sophia? When you dropped the baby off, why didn't you just tell me what was going on with you?"

"What could you have done?"

Mitch looked helpless. In retrospect, there wasn't a thing that he could've done for Sophia. He was just grateful now that she left the baby with him even though it ended his marriage to a woman he'd loved deeply and had wanted to spend the rest of his life with.

"I suppose the situation was far too much to carry alone yet it was impossible to share at that time. Do you understand?"

Mitch looked at Sophia a moment before he replied, "Yeah, I do. Absolutely I do." He looked down at his hands on the table.

"I am sure that for years you've been angry at me for one reason or another. The things I did to you the night we met, how forward I was, all those things I did to you when I was just a child, getting pregnant, and the fatal blow by looking you up and confronting you and your wife at your home.

What I did was unforgivable but," she paused a moment and cast her eyes towards the ceiling a moment before completing her statement, "I hope that in time you will be able to forgive me." Sophia paused again. "My therapist drilled into my head that I should forgive myself and although it took years, I finally got there. Mitch, what I am about to say is simply for your information. I did some terrible things and I am not going to place blame on anyone for my wrong doing. At sixteen, I was buck wild, I didn't have any real role models in my life. The home that I grew up in, the home where I was supposed to be loved, protected and where I was supposed to be safe, well in that home, I was exposed to the most deviant behaviors any child my age or any child for that matter, should've had to go through.

"My parents socialized…. a lot. They went on fabulous vacations, wonderful shopping trips, parties. It was what happened during the parties that changed my life forever. Yes, that was when it all started." Again, Sophia paused and looked away. Mitch remained quiet. Then Sophia looked at Mitch. "One night my parents were throwing one of their famous parties downstairs and I was asleep in my bed upstairs. At some point during the night, I was awakened by someone's hands touching me on my private parts. The lights were off and I couldn't see who was there with me. All I could hear was a man's voice whispering that I was to keep quiet, he wasn't going to hurt me, I was his pretty big girl. While my parents were going off to do naughty things, one of their friends was in the bedroom of their underage daughter and doing naughty things to her. Me. I told my parents what had happened to me but they discarded what I said, assuring me that I had an overactive imagination or that I was having bad dreams."

Mitch looked at Sophia in complete disbelief but he still remained quiet.

"Although this awful thing kept happening to me and I kept telling my parents, they didn't believe me. It was either that or they were too inebriated or engrossed in their own affairs to pay attention to what was going on with me, their only child, a female child. There were times when I would see my dad going off into one of the bedrooms with someone's wife and wouldn't come out until much later. I didn't know at the time what was going on but after a while, a lot of things made sense. As it turned out, I became familiar with Mr. Benjamin Mason's cologne. He used to wear a strong, repugnant cologne. When the folks would have friends over, Mr. Mason always wanted me to sit on his lap and believe it or not, My parents would encourage me to do it, not knowing that every chance he got when my parents' backs were turned, he was feeling me up. I remembered that same scent on him when he came into my bedroom at night. The abuse went on a couple of years and it only got worse."

Mitch exploded. He could no longer keep quiet, listening to how his beautiful Sophia was violated for years when she was a child. "What were your parents thinking? How could they not know what was happening to you? They had to have noticed the change in you. Well, when did the abuse stop and I hope your father kicked Mason's ass before having him thrown in jail," Mitch said, heatedly.

"No daddy didn't kick his ass nor did he have Mr. Mason arrested. He and Mom swept it under the rug and remained in a state of denial about that as they did most things that they refuse to face or would ruin their image in the community." Rubbing her hands together, Sophia looked at Mitch. "I don't know how long the molestation would have continued had Mr. Mason continued to put his mouth on me, but he went from that act to using his fingers to penetrate me. One day when Mom was giving me a bath and she was washing me there I began to scream. She took me to the doctor but she refused to name my perpetrator. After that, I never saw Mr. Mason from that time until last year when I was going into a drug store as he was leaving. He looked as if he'd seen a ghost."

"Did your parents get you some therapy to help you work through that terrible ordeal as much as was possible?" Mitch wanted to know.

"No. As I said, they wanted to keep it under the rug where they'd swept it."

"This just blows my mind."

"I know but when I turned 18, I put myself in therapy. I have a wonderful therapist who I've been seeing for years. I wanted to know why I behaved the way that I did; wild, loving the party life, but I wasn't promiscuous. I don't know what you think, but you were my first."

Mitch didn't say anything, but he knew that. He knew it the night he made love to Sophia.

"My therapist has been helping me to work through a lot of my issues and I am completely in touch with exactly who I am, I no longer blame myself solely for all the mistakes I made, and I've given myself permission to forgive myself."
"You should forgive yourself, considering all that you been through."

"So, what about your personal life."

"My personal life. You assume that I have one."

"Well, everyone has a personal life. It may not be all that we might want it to be. Well, is there someone special in your life? Are you married? Other kids?"

"By special I assume you mean do I have a significant other in my life. Well, the answer is no. I haven't had time to do fun. After having the baby, I got my high school diploma, then I went to New York University where I majored in Fashion and Psychology. Because I was so sick at times, I missed classes but I managed to graduate at the top of my class. So, as you can see, I really didn't have time for extracurricular activities." She paused. "I know I caused problems in your marriage and I am sorry about that. I have read things about her in the paper from time, but she has never been a real focus for me."

There wasn't anything left in Kaline that Mitch recognized anymore. He didn't respond.

"I know Mitch, Junior wouldn't remember me, but has he ever asked about me, you know, asked about his mommy?" Mitch didn't answer her. He stared at her, his brows knit. Although a sudden feeling of fear gripped her stomach, Sophia had to ask Mitch the question that had haunted her for years. She lifted her hands from her lap and placed them on the table with her fingers entwined. Her eyes met and held his. "When can I see him, Mitch?" she asked quietly.

He turned cold, stunned eyes on Sophia and looked at her for a long moment; then briefly he looked around the room, before he returned his attention back at her. "Are you hungry?"

"Mitch, you can't avoid my question. I want to see my baby, our baby. I want to be with him. I am well now and I want my child in my life."

"So now you want to take him away from me?"

"No, I don't want to do that but I know you and I can work something out that we can both be in Mitch, Junior's life. Please, Mitch. This is not a pity Sophia party. I am not waging no war on Sophia's rights." She paused a moment and her entire body shuddered. "I have missed my baby so much. Please," Sophia said and she began to cry.

Mitch took a deep breath. He removed a handkerchief from his pocket and handed it to her. "You don't have to cry. We will talk about it." He knew Sophia would want to see their son. They would just have to find a way to reintroduced her into Mitch, Junior's life without confusing him.

"You ready to order some dinner?"

"No, actually I'm not hungry. We had a late lunch, so I'm good."

"Great, because I've got an idea. Where are you staying?"

"Right here at the hotel."

"So am I. Let me make a suggestion."

"Sure. What?"

"Why don't we each go up and change and I'll take you out for the evening?"

Feeling a ripple of excitement rush through her body, Sophia said, "That's sounds great."

They got up from the table and after Mitch threw several bills on the table, they left the restaurant. When they entered the elevator, Mitch looked at Sophia before hitting a button for her floor. When she told him her suite was on the fourteenth floor, his mouth fell open. As luck or fate would have it, their rooms were on the same floor.

"This is too much of a coincidence," Sophia said and Mitch chuckled with her because he had to admit that it really was a coincidence. "I could not have scripted this better," she confessed.

Mitch looked at Sophia, completely amused by her as he took her room key card and opened the door to her suite. He was completely taken aback by Sophia's next move once the door was closed behind them. Sophia moved quickly into Mitch's arms and before he could think, she had fastened her arms around his neck and her tongue was in his mouth. Although the contact sent waves of sensual reaction crashing round his body, Mitch forced his mouth away from hers. And, staring at her lips, he gritted his teeth as he reached his hands up to Sophia's arms and removed them from around his neck ignoring the disappointed look on her face. Mitch looked at his watch. Six fifteen. "I'll pick you up at 8." With that, Mitch turned and walked out the door.

A strange sensation began deep in Mitch's stomach as he walked away from Sophia's door and down the corridor pass three room doors to his room. He removed his room key card from his pocket and opened the door to his room.

He entered the room, loosened his tie enough to pull it over his head and he threw it onto the bed along with his jacket. He kicked off his shoes, then his trousers. He went into the bathroom, turned on the shower, stepped into it and allowed the cold water to run over his head and down his tall, lean muscular body.

Mitch exited the bathroom with only a towel wrapped around him. He lay back on the bed, grabbed the remote and turned on the television. After flipping through the channels, not really paying attention to what was on the screen; Mitch turned off the set, leaped from the bed and ripped the towel from his body.

He unzipped his suitcase, pulled from it a white short sleeved pullover sweater and a pair of dark brown slacks that he hurried into. After ramming his feet into his shoes and slipping his room key card into his pants pocket, he rushed out of the room.
Although, initially he was still feeling some kind of way about Sophia, from the moment he laid eyes on her, spending time alone in his hotel room now was not very appealing.

As Mitch knocked on the room door, he was reminded that this situation felt like déjà vu all over again. Yes, it was déjà vu all over again and he didn't care. He didn't care six years ago and he doesn't care now.

Mitch interrupted Sophia taking a shower because when she opened the door, she had water beads on her face, her short copper hair was wet and matted against her head and she was wearing only a short white terrycloth robe.

Mitch pushed opened the door. Sophia looked up into his face, her beautiful enormous dark eyes dilated. Mitch grabbed Sophia and pulled her roughly into his arms as her robe fell open, exposing portions of her beautiful breasts. First, his mouth came down hard to meet her lips. He heard her intake of breath just before her tongue was in his mouth. The hunger that flared inside her matched his exactly.

While Mitch had one hand on Sophia's back to hold her body close to him, his other hand caught and held the back of her head, holding it captive so that she couldn't pull away even if she wanted to, and no way did Sophia want to; she was too engaged in kissing him back, her mouth moving ferociously and heatedly under his to do anything else.

He sucked hard on her tongue, wanting all of her sweetness deep inside his mouth. As the kiss deepened, a shudder of undeniable pleasure shot through her. Then, his tongue was inside her mouth and she used hers to toy with his. When their lips parted, his lips slid down her throat savoring the smell and taste of her freshly showered scented skin.

In one swift movement, Mitch lifted Sophia up into his arms and carried her over to her bed where he lay her down. Her robe completely open now, revealing her entire ripe, plump breasts caused Mitch's penis to press hard against the zipper of his slacks since he wasn't wearing underwear. His eyes never left hers as he ripped his sweater over his head, unzipped his pants and kicked them off along with his shoes. She gazed at him through heavy-lidded eyes filled with desire.

In the next moment, he was on the bed with Sophia in his arms. He kissed her and she kissed him back with all her hunger for love in her lips. After kissing her hard, bruising, he tore his mouth from hers, slid the robe down her arms, pulled it from her body and flung it to the floor. Now, they were naked. He moved his body against hers, skin to skin. She felt the course caress of his body hair, the heat and moisture between her thighs. She whispered his name, "Mitch." She ached for him to be inside her, to fill her as he'd done before, so long ago.

She wanted him so badly, needed him so much, she just had to have him, at least one more time. She was trembling when he buried his mouth between her breasts, whispering between kisses, "you're gonna drive me crazy you are so damn beautiful. I love looking at you. I love looking at your body." He took one of the hard beige aroused nipples into his mouth and sucked softly at it and then the other.

His mouth moved from her breasts back to her lips. When he had kissed her mouth thoroughly, his moist lips moved down her body, leaving a trail between her breasts, then to her navel. He used his tongue to tease the indented button. His next move even took him by surprise when his mouth claimed the spot between her inner thighs where he began to place hot, wet juicy kisses.

He used his mouth to bite, tease and nibble her until she could take no more. Sophia closed her eyes and groaned from the intense pleasure that he was igniting throughout her body. When it was like a crescendo of desire flowing through her, she screamed his name. Her body rose off the bed up against his face and she moved her body in such a way that let him know that she wanted him. All of him. "Are you ready for this," he asked.

Sophia was so touched by his concern for her that tears crept out under her lids. "Yes, my love. I'm fine and I'm ready for this. I'm ready for you."

He ran a finger over her closed eyes, gently wiping away the tears from her lashes. He kissed her once more as she spread her legs for him. When he entered her, he was certain he heard bells ringing in his ears. He made love to her gently yet thoroughly.

"Darling, I am a woman. Don't treat me like an expensive piece of china," she whispered against his mouth. "I am completely recovered and I want you to love me like I know you can."

Mitch didn't know how he was able to restrain himself as long as he did but now that she was giving him permission to take her as he wanted to, his passion mounted in a way that he had never experienced before and he unleashed pent up feelings that had gone untouched in that way for years and all he wanted to do was swim in her in her body for the rest of his life.

When they awoke hours after being wrapped in each other's arms, Sophia said, "I knew you were coming back here."

"No you didn't," Mitch teased but he believed that somehow she did know. She had such intuition into him and his behavior. Hadn't she predicted that they would make love together almost six years ago, walking on the beach on Myrtle Beach?

Sophia pulled her head back so that she could look into his eyes. He smiled as he stared down into her beautiful face and he wondered what it would be like to journey through the seasons of life with her. Mitch then pulled her head back close to him. So much had happened within the past twenty-four hours, so much and the strangest feeling had come over him. Now that she was back in his arms, he wanted her to stay. He whispered against her hair, "We've got so much to talk about and some tough decisions to make."

Sophia responded, "I agree!"

"I don't know how you feel about this but I don't what to lose you again. Six years ago, there wasn't anything I could do about it even if I wanted to. But now I can, but only if you want me as much as I want you."

Sophia remained silent.

"I would like nothing more than to have you, our son and I together as a family."

It was Sophia's turn to speak. "What exactly are you saying?"

"Call me crazy, Sophia but I want you to marry me."

"I believe I loved you from the night we first met but when the situation went so far out of control, I just stored my feelings for you in the deep recesses of my mind.

Though it came out of nowhere, after making up his mind to ask Sophia to marry him, Mitch was impatient for an answer. "Well…Sophia? Will you marry me? Will you marry us?"

Mitch knew that time didn't heal everything. Some things that happen in life never heal. Sometimes the pain of a particular situation goes on forever. He didn't know where time would take him, Mitch Jr. and Sophia, but he was certain he was willing to go on that journey with Sophia and their son and see where it lead.

"Yes! Yes! I will marry you! I have been waiting for you to ask me from the time when we first met." Sophia knew the first night she saw Mitch that she was going to meet him. And, though she didn't know how she would make it happen, she knew she was going to have him. Somehow she just knew it. She was thirsty for Mitch then. She was thirsty for him now. Sophia's wish had come true. Her wish upon that falling star that night long ago, her sin and her shame were now things of the past. Then suddenly Sophia leaped out of bed.

"Where are you going," Mitch asked.

Sophia didn't answer him. She went over to her suitcase, searched through it and after removing something, she walked back over and got back into bed with Mitch.

"What have you got there?" Mitch was curious.

Sophia revealed to him what she was holding in her hand.

Mitch's face broke out into a huge grin. "A seashell." He took the seashell from Sophia's hand, looked at it, then he looked at her. "This is the seashell I gave you on the beach that night all those years ago." It was a statement not a question.

"Yes, it is."

"You kept it."

"I told you I would."

Mitch knew at that moment that he had not nor would he ever love another woman as he loved Sophia, and he knew he always would. "I love you, baby," he said. "And I can't wait to take you home to see our son."

Sophia was so excited she could hardly breathe. "I love you, Mitch."

Mitch took Sophia into his arms and he kissed her and kissed her. He kissed his beautiful, sweet woman with a passion that he had not felt since the first night they met.

www.ingramcontent.com/pod-product-compliance
Lightning Source LLC
Chambersburg PA
CBHW031612240626
47153CB00002B/732